LOUIS L'AMOUR

We look to Louis L'Amour for the finest writing about the American West. Here, written with all of the sheer storytelling power we have come to expect of Louis L'Amour, is a different and very special book.

YONDERING contains adventures of the sea, of war, of the exotic islands of the East, stories based upon experiences and people L'Amour encountered in his early yondering days.

Most of the men and women of YONDERING do not face their challenges in the old West, yet they summon up courage and strengths that would have stood them well on the American frontier. They discover, as L'Amour discovered in his own past, that in the daily act of survival, each of us conquers his own frontiers.

YONDERING

Bantam Books by Louis L'Amour
Ask your bookseller for the books you have missed

NOVELS

BENDIGO SHAFTER
BORDEN CHANTRY
BRIONNE
THE BROKEN GUN
THE BURNING HILLS
THE CALIFORNIOS
CALLAGHEN
CATLOW
CHANCY
THE CHEROKEE TRAIL
COMSTOCK LODE
CONAGHER
CROSSFIRE TRAIL
DARK CANYON
DOWN THE LONG HILLS
THE EMPTY LAND
FAIR BLOWS THE WIND
FALLON
THE FERGUSON RIFLE
THE FIRST FAST DRAW
FLINT
GUNS OF THE TIMBERLANDS
HANGING WOMAN CREEK
THE HAUNTED MESA
HELLER WITH A GUN
THE HIGH GRADERS
HIGH LONESOME
HONDO
HOW THE WEST WAS WON
THE IRON MARSHAL
THE KEY-LOCK MAN
KID RODELO
KILKENNY
KILLOE
KILRONE
KIOWA TRAIL
LAST OF THE BREED
LAST STAND AT PAPAGO WELLS
THE LONESOME GODS
THE MAN CALLED NOON
THE MAN FROM SKIBBEREEN
THE MAN FROM THE BROKEN HILLS
MATAGORDA
MILO TALON
THE MOUNTAIN VALLEY WAR
NORTH TO THE RAILS
OVER ON THE DRY SIDE
PASSIN' THROUGH
THE PROVING TRAIL
THE QUICK AND THE DEAD
RADIGAN
REILLY'S LUCK
THE RIDER OF LOST CREEK
RIVERS WEST
THE SHADOW RIDERS
SHALAKO
SHOWDOWN AT YELLOW BUTTE

SILVER CANYON
SITKA
SON OF A WANTED MAN
TAGGART
THE TALL STRANGER
TO TAME A LAND
TUCKER
UNDER THE SWEETWATER RIM
UTAH BLAINE
THE WALKING DRUM
WESTWARD THE TIDE
WHERE THE LONG GRASS BLOWS

SHORT STORY COLLECTIONS

BOWDRIE
BOWDRIE'S LAW
BUCKSKIN RUN
DUTCHMAN'S FLAT
THE HILLS OF HOMICIDE
LAW OF THE DESERT BORN
LONIGAN
NIGHT OVER THE SOLOMONS
THE RIDER OF THE RUBY HILLS
RIDING FOR THE BRAND
THE STRONG SHALL LIVE
THE TRAIL TO CRAZY MAN
WAR PARTY
WEST FROM SINGAPORE
YONDERING

SACKETT TITLES

SACKETT'S LAND
TO THE FAR BLUE MOUNTAINS
THE WARRIOR'S PATH
JUBAL SACKETT
RIDE THE RIVER
THE DAYBREAKERS
SACKETT
LANDO
MOJAVE CROSSING
MUSTANG MAN
THE LONELY MEN
GALLOWAY
TREASURE MOUNTAIN
LONELY ON THE MOUNTAIN
RIDE THE DARK TRAIL
THE SACKETT BRAND
THE SKY-LINERS

NONFICTION

FRONTIER
THE SACKETT COMPANION:
A Personal Guide to the
Sackett Novels
A TRAIL OF MEMORIES:
The Quotations of Louis L'Amour,
compiled by Angelique L'Amour

YONDERING

LOUIS L'AMOUR

BANTAM BOOKS
NEW YORK · TORONTO · LONDON · SYDNEY · AUCKLAND

YONDERING

A Bantam Book / June 1980
15 printings through December 1988

ISBN 0-553-28104-6

Published simultaneously in the United States and Canada

*Bantam Books are published by Bantam Books, a division of Bantam Doubleday
Dell Publishing Group, Inc. Its trademark, consisting of the words "Bantam
Books" and the portrayal of a rooster, is Registered in U.S. Patent and Trade-
mark Office and in other countries. Marca Registrada. Bantam Books, 666
Fifth Avenue, New York, New York 10103.*

PRINTED IN THE UNITED STATES OF AMERICA

KR   24   23   22   21   20   19   18   17

To Marc Jaffe . . .
A good friend
and a fine gentleman
from New York
whom I met in a saloon
in Elko, Nevada.

Somewhere my love lay sleeping
    Behind the lights of a far-off town;
So I gave my heart to a bend in the road,
    And off I went, a-yondering.

CONTENTS

INTRODUCTION

IN THE BEGINNING there was a dream, a young boy's dream, a dream of far lands to see, of oceans to cross, and somewhere at the trail's end, a girl. *The girl*.

More than all else I wanted to tell stories, stories that people could read or hear, stories to love and remember. I had no desire to write to please those who make it their business to comment but for the people who do the work of the world, who live on the land or love the land, people who make and bake and struggle to make ends meet, for the people who invent, who design, who build, for the people who do. And if somewhere down the line a man or woman can put a finger on a line and say, "Yes, that is the way it was. I was there," then I would be amply repaid.

I have never scoffed at sentiment. Cynicism is ever the outward face of emptiness.

What, after all, is romance? It is the music of those who make the world turn, the people who make things happen. Romance is the story of dreams that could come true and so often do.

Why do men ride the range? Go to sea? Explore the polar icecaps? Why do they ride rockets to unknown worlds? It is because of romance, because of the stories they have read and the stories they have dreamed.

Some have said this is the age of the nonhero, that the day of the hero is gone. That's nonsense. When the hero is gone, man himself will be gone, for the hero is our future, our destiny.

These are some of the stories of a writer trying to

find his way, trying to find the truth of what he has seen, to understand the people, to learn a little more about telling a story.

The people whom I have met and with whom I worked in those earlier years were not always nice people, but each in his own way was strong, or he could not survive. Of course, there were some who did not, some who could not survive. For one reason or another, nature weeded them out and cast them aside, just as happened on our frontier during the westward movement.

Some of these stories are from my own life; some are from the lives of people I met along the way.

WHERE THERE'S FIGHTING

In the passing of time when greater events occupy the attention of the world, some things are forgotten that should be remembered. The following story is just one tiny tribute to many gallant men, both British and Greek, who attempted to stay, if just for a little while, what was at the time an invincible tide.

On about April 6, 1941 Germany invaded Greece as one small fragment of a much larger pattern. Anticipating such a move, Great Britain had landed 57,000 men under Gen. Maitland Wilson. Moving with speed and efficiency, the German armored divisions struck south, and between April twelfth and the twentieth German spearheads advanced through the rugged mountain terrain of central Greece.

Papagos, realizing victory was impossible, suggested he try to stay the advance long enough for the British forces to escape intact so they could fight elsewhere. His efforts were so successful that despite a German parachute drop near Corinth, some 43,000 British soldiers were evacuated. Many of these soldiers were with Alexander when he won his victory in North Africa.

The story here is an episode in the German advance through the mountains of central Greece.

THE FOUR MEN were sprawled in a cuplike depression at the top of the pass. From where the machine gun was planted it had a clear field of fire for over four hundred yards. Beyond that the road was visible only at intervals. By a careful watch of those intervals an enemy could be seen long before he was within range.

A low parapet of loose rock had been thrown up along the lip of the depression, leaving an aperture for the .30-caliber gun. Two of the men were also armed with rifles.

It was very still. The slow warmth of the morning sun soaked into their bones and ate the frost away, leaving them lethargic and pleased. The low rumble as of thunder in the far-off hills were the bombs over Serbia, miles away.

"Think they'll ever come?" Benton asked curiously.

"They'll come," Ryan said.

"We can't stop them."

"No."

"How about some coffee? Is there any left?"

Ryan nodded. "It'll be ready soon. The part that's coffee is done, the part that's chicory is almost done, and the part that's plain bean is doing."

Benton looked at the two who were sleeping in the sun. They were mere boys. "Shall we wake them?"

"Pretty soon. They worry too much. Especially Pommy. He's afraid of being afraid."

"Sackworth doesn't. He thinks we're bloody heroes. Do you?"

3

"I'd feel heroic as blazes if I had a shave," Ryan said. "Funny, how you like being shaved. It sets a man up somehow."

Pommy turned over and opened his eyes. "I say, Bent? Shall I spell you a bit? You've been there hours!"

Benton looked at him, liking his fresh, clean-cut look.

"I could use some coffee. I feel like I was growing to this rock."

The young Englishman had risen to his feet.

"There's something coming down there. A man, I think."

"Couldn't be one of our men. We didn't have any over there. He's stopped—looking back."

"He's coming on again now," Sackworth said after a moment. He had joined them at the first sign of trouble. "Shall I try a shot?"

"Wait. Might be a Greek."

The sun climbed higher, and the moving figure came slowly toward them. He seemed to move at an almost creeping pace. At times, out of sight of the pass, they thought he would never show up again.

"He's carrying something," Pommy said. "Too heavy for a rifle, but I saw the sun flash on it back there a way."

The man came into sight around the last bend. He was big, but he walked very slowly, limping a little. He was wearing faded khaki trousers and a torn shirt. Over one shoulder were several belts of ammunition.

"He hasn't carried that very far," Ryan said. "He's got over a hundred pounds there."

Benton picked up one of the rifles and stepped to the parapet, but before he could lift the gun or speak, the man looked up. Benton thought he had never seen a face so haggard with weariness. It was an utter and complete weariness that seemed to come from within. The man's face was covered with a stubble of black beard. His face was wide at the cheekbones, and the nose was broken. His head was wrapped in a bloody bandage above which coarse black hair was visible.

"Any room up there?" he asked.

"Who are you?" Benton demanded.

Without replying, the big man started up the steep path. Once he slipped, skinning his knee against a sharp rock. Puzzled, they waited. When he stood beside them, they were shocked at his appearance. His face, under the deep brown of sun and wind, was drawn and pale, his nose peeling from sunburn. The rags of what must have once been a uniform were mud stained and sweat discolored.

"What difference does it make?" he asked mildly, humorously. "I'm here now."

He lowered the machine gun and slid the belts to the ground. When he straightened, they could see he was a half inch taller than Benton, who was a tall man, and at least thirty pounds heavier. Through his shirt bulging muscles showed, and there was blood clogging the hair on his chest.

"My name's Horne," he added. "Mike Horne. I've been fighting with Koska's guerrillas in Albania."

Benton stared, uncertain. "Albania? That's a long way from here."

"Not so far if you know the mountains." He looked at the pot on the fire. "How's for some coffee?"

Silently Ryan filled a cup. Digging in his haversack, Horne produced some Greek bread and a thick chunk of sausage. He brushed the sand from the sausage gravely. "Want some? I salvaged this from a bombed house back yonder. Might be some shell fragments in it."

"You pack that gun over the mountains?" Ryan asked.

Horne nodded, his mouth full. "Part of the way. It was surrounded by dead Greeks when I found it. Four Italians found it the same time. We had trouble."

"Did you—kill them all?" Pommy asked.

Horne looked at him. "No, kid. I asked them to tea an' then put sand in their bearings."

Pommy's face got red; then he grinned.

"Got any ammo for a .50?" Horne looked up at Benton. "I got mighty little left."

"They put down four boxes by mistake," Benton said.

Ryan was interested. "Koska's guerrillas? I heard of them. Are they as tough as you hear?"

"Tougher. Koska's an Albanian gypsy. Sneaked into Valona alone a few nights ago an' got himself three dagos. With a knife."

Sackworth studied Horne as if he were some kind of insect. "You call that bravery? That's like animals. One can at least fight like a gentleman!"

Horne winked at Ryan. "Sure, kid. But this ain't a gentleman's fight. This is war. Nothing sporting about it, just a case of dog eat dog, an' you better have big teeth."

"Why are you here?" Sackworth demanded.

Horne shrugged. "Why am I any place? Think I'm a fifth columnist or something?" He stared regretfully into the empty cup. "Well, I'm not. I ran a gun in the Chaco a few years ago; then they started to fight in China, so I went there. I was in the Spanish scrap with the Loyalists.

"Hung around in England long enough to learn something about that parachute business. Now that's a man's job. When you get down in an enemy country, you're on your own. I was with the bunch that hopped off from Libya and parachuted down in southern Italy to cut off that aqueduct and supply line to the Sicily naval base. Flock of 'spiggoties' spotted me, but I got down to the water and hiked out in a fishing boat. Now I'm here."

He looked up at Benton, wiping the back of his

hand across his mouth. "From Kalgoorlie, I bet. You got the look. I prospected out of there once. I worked for pearls out of Darwin, too. I'm an original swag man, friend."

"What's a swag man?" Pommy asked.

Horne looked at him, smiling. Two of his front teeth at the side were missing.

"It's a bum, sonny. Just a bum. A guy who packs a tucker bag around looking for whatever turns up."

Horne pulled the gun over into his lap, carefully wiping the oil buffer clean. Then he oiled the moving parts of the gun with a little can he took from his hip pocket and slowly assembled it. He handled the gun like a lover, fitting the parts together smoothly and testing it carefully for head space when it was ready for firing.

"That a German shirt you have on?" Sackworth asked. His eyes were level, and he had his rifle across his knees, pointed at Horne.

"Sure," Horne said mildly. "I needed a shirt, so I took it out of a dead German's outfit."

"Looting," Sackworth said with scorn. There was distaste and dislike in his gaze.

"Why not?" Horne looked up at Sackworth, amused. "You're a good kid, so don't start throwing your weight around. This sportsmanship stuff, the old school tie, an' whatnot—that's okay where it belongs. You Britishers who play war like a game are living in the past. There's nothing sporting about this. It's like waterfronts or jungles. You survive any way you can."

Sackworth did not move the rifle. "I don't like him," he said to Benton. "I don't trust him."

"Forget it!" Benton snapped. "The man's all right, and Lord knows we need fighting men!"

"Sure," Horne added quietly. "It's just you an' me are different kind of animals, kid. You're probably Eton and then Sandhurst. Me, I came up the hard way. A tough road kid in the States, then an able seaman, took a whirl at the fight game, and wound up in Chaco.

"I like to fight. I also like to live. I been in a lot of fights, and mostly I fought pretty good, an' I'm still alive. The Jerries use whatever tactics they need. What you need, kid, in war is not a lot of cut an' dried rules but a good imagination, the ability to use what you've got to the best advantage no matter where you are, and a lot of the old moxie.

"You'll make a good fighter. You got the moxie. All you need is a little kicking around."

"I wish we knew where the Jerries were," Ryan said. "This waiting gets me."

"You'll see them pretty quick," Horne said. "There's about a battalion in the first group, and there's only one tank."

Benton lowered his cup, astonished. "You mean you've actually seen them? They are coming?"

Horne nodded. "The main body isn't far behind the first bunch."

"Why didn't you say so?" Sackworth demanded. His face was flushed and angry. "We could have warned the troops behind us."

"Yeah?" Horne did not look up from wiping the dust from the cartridges. "Well, we couldn't. You see," he added, looking up, "they broke through Monastir Pass two days ago. Your men back there know more about it than we do. This is just a supporting column to polish off any leftovers like us."

"Then—we're cut off?" Pommy asked.

Horne nodded. "You have been for two days. How long you been here?"

"Just three days," Benton said. He studied Horne thoughtfully. "What are you? A Yank?"

Horne shrugged. "I guess so. When I joined up in Spain, they took my citizenship away. It was against the law to fight fascism then. If it was wrong then, it's wrong now. But me, I feel just the same. I'll fight them in China, in Spain, in Africa, or anywhere else.

"In Spain when everything was busting up, I heard about this guy Koska. One of his men was with us, so when he went back, I trailed along."

"They're coming," Sackworth said. "I can see the tank."

"All right," Benton said. He finished his coffee.

"Did you fight any Germans in Spain?" Pommy asked.

"Yeah." Mike Horne brushed invisible dust from the gun and fed a belt of cartridges into it. "Most of them aren't much better than the Italians. They fight better—the younger ones try harder—but all they know how to do is die."

"It's something to know that," Sackworth said.

"Nuts. Anybody can die. Everybody does. And dead soldiers never won any battles. The good soldier is the one who keeps himself alive and fighting. This bravery stuff—that's for milksops. For pantywaists. All of us are scared, but we fight just the same."

"The tank's getting closer," Sackworth said. He was plainly worried and showed it.

"I got the .50," Horne said. He settled himself comfortably into the sand and moved his gun on the swivel. "Let it get closer. Don't fire until they are close up to us. I'll take the tank. You take the first truck with the other gun, I'll take the second, an' so on. Get the drivers if you can."

They were silent. The rumble of the tank and heavy clank of the tread drew nearer. Behind them rolled the trucks, the men sitting in tight groups. They apparently expected no trouble.

"I'd have expected them to send a patrol," Benton said, low voiced.

"They did," Horne replied.

They looked at him, startled. His eyes were on the gray-green column. He had sighted the fifty at the gun aperture on the tank.

"All right," he said suddenly.

His gun broke into a hoarse chatter, slamming steel-jacketed bullets at the tank. Then its muzzle lifted suddenly and swept the second truck. Soldiers were shouting and yelling, spilling from trucks like madmen, but the two first trucks were smashed into carriers of death before the men could move. The Germans farther back had found their enemy, and steel-jacketed bullets smashed into the parapet. Pommy felt something like a hot whiplash along his jaw.

They were above the column and out of reach of the tank. Mike Horne stood up suddenly and depressed the gun muzzle. The tank was just below. The gun chattered, and the tank slewed around sideways and drove full tilt into the rock wall as though to climb it.

Horne dropped back. "The older ones have a soft spot on top," he said.

The men of the broken column ran for shelter. Some of them tried to rush the steep path, but the fire blasted them back to the road, dead or dying. Others, trying to escape the angry bursts from the two guns, tried to scramble up the walls of the pass but were mowed down relentlessly.

It had been a complete and shocking surprise. The broken column became a rout. Horne stopped the .50 and wiped his brow with the back of his hand. He winked at Ryan.

"Nice going, kid. That's one tank that won't bother your pals."

Ryan peered around the rocks. The pass was empty of life. The wrecked tank was jammed against the rock wall, and one of the trucks had plunged off the precipice into the ravine. Another was twisted across the road.

A man was trying to get out of the first truck. He

made it and tumbled to the road. His coat was stained with blood, and he was making whimpering sounds and trying to crawl. His face and head were bloody.

"Next time it'll be tough," Horne said. "They know now. They'll come in small bunches, scattered out, running for shelter behind the trucks."

Rifle fire began to sweep over the cup. They were low behind the parapet and out of sight. It was a searching, careful fire—expert fire.

Benton was quiet. He looked over at Horne. Officially in charge, he had yielded his command to Horne's superior knowledge.

"What d'you think?" he asked.

"We'll stop them," Horne said. "We'll stop them this time, maybe next time. After that—"

Horne grinned at Pommy. "First time under fire?"

"Yes."

"Take it easy. You're doing all right. Make every shot count. One cinch is worth five maybes."

Pommy crowded his body down into the gravel and rested his rifle in a niche in the rocks. He looked at Mike Horne and could see a thin trickle of fresh blood coming from under his bandage. The wound had opened again.

Was it deep, he wondered, or just a scratch? He looked at the lines about Horne's mouth and decided it was deep. Horne's sleeve was torn, and he had a dragon tattooed on his forearm.

They came with a rush. Rounding the bend, they broke into a scattered line; behind them, machine guns and rifles opened a hot fire to cover the advance.

They waited, and just before the men could reach the trucks, swept them with a steel scythe of bullets that mowed them down in a row. One man tumbled off the brink and fell into the ravine; then another fell, caught his fingers on the lip, and tumbled head over heels into the ravine as the edge gave way.

"How many got there?" Horne asked.

"A dozen, I think," Ryan said. "We got about thirty."

"Fair enough." Horne looked at Sackworth. The young Englishman was still resentful. He didn't like Horne. "Doing all right?" Horne asked.

"Of course." Sackworth was contemptuous, but his face was drawn and gray.

"Ryan," Horne said, "you and Pommy leave the main attack to the machine guns. Watch the men behind the trucks. Pick them off as they try to move closer. You take the right, Pommy."

The German with the bloody face had fallen flat. Now he was getting to his knees again.

Then, suddenly, three men made a concerted rush. Ryan and Pommy fired instantly, and Ryan's man dropped.

"I missed!" Pommy said. "Blast it, I missed!"

There was another rush, and both machine guns broke into a clattering roar. The gray line melted away, but more kept coming. Men rounded the bend and split to the right and left. Despite the heavy fire a few of them were getting through. Pommy and Ryan were firing continuously and methodically now.

Suddenly a man broke from under the nearest truck and came on in a plunging rush. Both Ryan and Pommy fired, and the man went down, but before they could fire again, he lunged to his feet and dove into the hollow below the cliff on which their pit rested.

"He can't do anything there," Sackworth said. "He—"

A hurtling object shot upward from below, hit the slope below the guns, rolled a few feet, and then burst with an earth-shaking concussion.

Horne looked up from where he had ducked his head. Nobody was hit.

"He's got grenades. Watch it. There'll be another in a minute."

Ryan fired, and a man dropped his rifle and started back toward the trucks. He walked quite calmly while they stared. Then he fell flat and didn't get up.

Twice more grenades hit the slope, but the man was too close below the cliff. They didn't quite reach the cup thrown from such an awkward angle. "If one of those makes it—" Benton looked sour.

Pommy was shooting steadily now. There was another rush, and Benton opened up with the machine gun. Suddenly another grenade came up from below, traveling an arching course. It hit the slope, too short. It rolled free and fell. There was a terrific explosion.

"Tough," Ryan said. "He made a good try."

"Yeah," Horne said. "So have we."

Hours passed. The machine guns rattled steadily now. Only at long intervals was there a lull. The sun had swung over and was setting behind the mountain.

Horne straightened, his powerful body heavy with fatigue. He looked over at Ryan and grinned. Ryan's face was swollen from the kick of the rifle. Benton picked up a canteen and tried to drink, but there was no water.

"What now?" Pommy said.

Horne shrugged. "We take it on the lam."

"What?" Sackworth demanded. "What does that mean?"

"We beat it," Mike Horne said. "We get out while the getting is good."

"What?" Sackworth was incredulous. "You mean— *run?* Leave our post?"

"That's just what I mean," Horne said patiently. "We delayed this bunch long enough. We got ours from them, but now it doesn't matter anymore. The Jerries are behind us now. We delayed them for a while. All around through these hills guys are delaying them just for a while. We've done all we could here. Now we scram. We fight somewhere else."

"Go if you want to," Sackworth said stubbornly. "I'm staying."

Suddenly there was a terrific concussion, then another and another.

"What the deuce?" Benton exclaimed. "They got a mortar. They—"

The next shell hit right where he was sitting. It went off with an ear-splitting roar and a burst of flame. Pommy went down, hugged the earth with an awful fear. Something tore at his clothes; then sand and gravel showered over him. There was another concussion and another.

Somebody had caught him by the foot. "Come on, kid. Let's go."

They broke into a stumbling run down the slope back of the nest, then over the next ridge and down the ravine beyond. Even then they ran on, using every bit of cover. Once Pommy started to slow, but Horne nudged him with the rifle barrel.

"Keep it up," he panted. "We got to run."

They slid into a deeper ravine and found their way to a stream. They walked then, slipping and sliding in the gathering darkness. Once a patrol saw them, and shots rattled around, but they kept going.

Then it was night, and clouds covered the moon and the stars. Wearily, sodden with exhaustion, they plodded on. Once, on the bank of a little stream, they paused for a drink. Then Horne opened the old haversack again and brought out the remnants of the sausage and bread. He broke each in half, and shared them with Pommy.

"But—"

Pommy's voice caught in his throat. "Gone?" he said then.

Horne nodded in the darkness. "Yeah. Lucky it wasn't all of us."

"But what now?" Pommy asked. "You said they were behind us."

"Sure," Horne agreed. "But we're just two men. We'll travel at night, keep to the hills. Maybe they'll make a stand at Thermopylae. If not there, they might try to defend the Isthmus of Corinth. Maybe we can join them there."

"But if they don't? If we can't?"

"Then Africa, Pommy, or Syria or Suez or Russia or England. They'll always be fighting them somewhere, an' that's where I want to be. It won't stop. The Germans win here, they win there, but they got to keep on fighting. They win battles, but none of them are decisive. None of them mean an end.

"Ever fight a guy, kid, who won't quit? You keep kicking him, and he keeps coming back for more, keeps trying. You knock him down, but he won't stay down? It's hell, that's what it is. He won't quit, so you can't.

"But they'll be fighting them somewhere, and that's where I want to be."

"Yeah," Pommy said. "Me, too."

THE DANCING
KATE

For those interested, the reef in this story is
Pocklington, and its location has been described
in the story itself.

Misima Island is one of the Louisiade Archipel-
ago, an extensive chain. Many of these islands
are quite mountainous and rugged of aspect.
They are heavily forested. Both alluvial and reef
gold have been found there, as implied in the
story.

Until a few years ago the natives among the
eastern islands were reputed to be cannibals,
but according to the latest reports this is no
longer true, if it ever was.

It is rarely beautiful chain of islands, pictur-
esque and relatively untouched.

I T WAS A STRIP of grayish-yellow sand caught in the gaunt fingers of the reef like the upturned belly except here and there where the reef had been longest above the sea. Much of the reef was drying, and elsewhere the broken teeth of the coral formed ugly ridges flanked by a few black, half-submerged boulders.

At one end of the bar the stark white ribs of an old ship thrust themselves from the sand, and nearby lay the rusting hulk of an iron freighter. It had been there more than sixty years.

For eighteen miles in a northeast and southwest direction the reef lay across the face of the Coral Sea. At its widest, no more than three miles but narrowing to less than a mile. A strip of jagged coral and white water lost in the remote emptiness of the Pacific. The long dun swells of the sea hammered against the outer rocks, and overhead the towering vastness of the sky became a shell of copper with the afternoon sun.

At the near end of the bar, protected from the breaking seas in all but a hurricane, a hollow of rock formed a natural cistern. In the bottom were a few scant inches of doubtful water. Beside it, he squatted in torn dungarees and battered sneakers.

"Three days," he estimated, staring into the cistern, eyes squinting against the surrounding glare. "Three days if I'm careful, and after that I'm washed up."

After that—thirst. The white, awful glare of the tropical sun, a parched throat, baking flesh, a few days or hours of delirium, and then a long time of lying wide-eyed to the sky before the gulls and the crabs finished the remains.

He had no doubt as to where he was. The chart had been given him in Port Darwin and was worn along the creases, but there was no crease where this reef lay, hence no doubt of his position. He was sitting on a lonely reef, avoided by shipping, right in the middle of nowhere. His position was approximately 10°45′ S, 155°51′ E.

The nearest land was eighty-two miles off and it might as well be eighty-two thousand.

It started with the gold. The schooner on which he had been second mate had dropped anchor in Bugoiya Harbor, but it was not fit anchorage, so they could remain only a matter of hours. He was on the small wharf superintending the loading of some cargo when a boy approached him.

He was a slender native boy with very large, beautiful eyes. When the boy was near him, he spoke, not looking at him. "Man say you come. Speak nobody."

"Come? Come where?"

"You come. I show you."

"I'm busy, boy. I don't want a girl now."

"No girl. Man die soon. He say *please*, you come?"

Dugan looked at his watch. They were loading the last cargo now, but they would not sail for at least an hour.

"How far is it?"

"Ten minutes—you see."

A man was dying? But why come to him? Still, in these islands odd things were always happening, and he was a curious man.

The captain was coming along the wharf, and he walked over to him. "Cap? Something's come up. This boy wants to take me to some man who is dying. Says not to say anything, and he's only ten minutes away."

Douglas glanced at the boy, then at his watch. "All right, but we've less than an hour. If we leave before you get back, we'll be several days at Woodlark or Murua or whatever they call it. There's a man in a village who is a friend of mine. Just ask for Sam. He will sail you over there."

"No need for that. I'll be right back."

Douglas glanced at him, a faint humor showing. "Dugan, I've been in these islands for fifty years. A man never knows—never."

Misima, although only about twenty miles long and four or five miles wide, was densely wooded, and the mountains lifted from a thousand to three thousand feet, and as the south side was very steep, most of the villages were along the northern shore.

The boy had walked off and was standing near a palm tree idly tossing stones into the lagoon. Taking off his cap, he walked away from the wharf, wiping the sweat from his brow. He walked back from the shore and then turned and strolled toward the shade, pausing occasionally. The boy had disappeared under the trees.

At the edge of the trees Dugan sat down, leaning his back against one. After a moment a stone landed near his foot, and he glimpsed the boy behind a tree about thirty yards off. Dugan got up, stretched, and hands in his pockets, strolled along in the shade, getting deeper and deeper until he saw the boy standing in a little-used path.

They walked along for half a mile. Dugan glanced at his watch. He would have to hurry.

Suddenly the boy ducked into the brush, holding a branch aside for him. About thirty yards away he saw a small shanty with a thin column of smoke lifting it. The boy ran ahead, leading the way.

There was a young woman there who, from her looks, was probably the boy's mother. Inside, an old man lay on an army cot. His eyes were sunken into his head, and his cheeks were gaunt. He clutched Dugan's hand. His fingers were thin and clawlike. "You must help me. You are with Douglas?"

"I am."

"Good! He is honest. Everybody knows that of him. I need your help." He paused for a minute, his breathing hoarse and labored. "I have a granddaughter. She is in Sydney." He put his hand on a coarse brown sack under his cot. "She must have this."

"What is it?"

"It is gold. There are men here who will steal it when I die. It must go to my granddaughter. You take it to her, and you keep half. You will do this?"

Sydney? He was not going to Sydney; still, one could sell it and send the money to Sydney. He pressed a paper into his hand. "Her name and address. Get it to her—somehow. You can do it. You will do it."

"Look," he protested, "I am not going to Sydney. When I leave Douglas, I'm going to Singapore and catch a ship for home—or going on to India."

"You must! They will steal it. They have tried, and they are waiting. If they think you have it, they will rob you. I know them."

"Well." He hesitated. He had to be getting back. Douglas's appointment at Woodlark was important to him. He would wait for no man in such a case, least of all for me, who had been with him only a few weeks, the man thought. "All right, give me the gold. I've little time."

The woman dragged the sack from under the cot, and he stooped to lift it. It was much heavier than it appeared. The old man smiled. "Gold is always heavy, my friend. Too heavy for many men to bear."

Dugan straightened and took the offered hand; then he walked out of the shack, carrying the gold.

It *was* heavy. Once aboard the schooner it would be no problem. He glanced at his watch and swore. He was already too late, and the tide—

When he reached the small harbor, it was too late. The schooner was gone!

He stood, staring. Immediately he was apprehensive. He was left on an island with about two dozen white people of whom he knew nothing and some fifteen hundred natives of whom he knew less. Moreover, there was always a drifting population, off the vessels of one kind or another that haunt Indonesian seas.

Woodlark was eighty miles away. He knew that much depended on the schooner being there in time to complete a deal for cargo that otherwise would go to another vessel. He had been left behind. He was alone.

A stocky bearded man approached. He wore dirty khakis, a watch cap, and the khaki coat hung loose. Did he have a gun? Dugan would have bet that he had.

From descriptions he was sure he knew the man.

"Looks like they've gone off and left you," he commented, glancing at the sack.

"They'll be back."

"Douglas? Don't bet on it. He calls in here about once every six months. Sometimes it's a whole year."

"It's different this time," he lied. "He's spending about three months in the Louisiades and Solomons. He expects to be calling in here three or four times, so I'll just settle down and wait."

"We could make a deal," the man said. "I could sail you to the Solomons." He jerked his head. "I've got a good boat, and I often take the trip. Come along."

"Why? When he's coming back here?"

Deliberately he turned his back and walked away. Zimmerman—this would be Zimmerman.

At the trade store they told him where he could find Sam, and he found him, a wiry little man with sad blue eyes and thin hair. He shook his head. "I have to live here."

"Douglas said—"

"I can imagine. I like Douglas. He's one of the best men in the islands, but he doesn't live here. I do. If you get out of here, you'll do it on your own. I can tell you something else. Nobody will take the chance. You make a deal with them, or you wait until Douglas comes back."

Twice he saw the boy, and he was watching him. He lingered near the trees where he'd been when he first followed him, so he started back. He'd have to see the old man, and packing that gold was getting to be a nuisance.

When he got back to the shack, the woman was at the door, mashing something in a wooden dish. "He's dying," she said. "He hasn't talked since you left."

"Who is it?" The voice was very weak.

He went inside and told the old man he would have to leave his gold. The schooner was gone, and he had no way to get to Woodlark and overtake her.

"Take my boat," he said.

His eyes closed, and nothing Dugan said brought any response. And Dugan tried. He wanted to get away, but he wanted no more of his gold. From Sam's manner he knew Zimmerman was trouble, very serious trouble.

The woman was standing there. "He is dying," she said.

"He has a boat?"

She pointed and he walked through the trees to the shore. It was there, tied up to a small boat dock. It wasn't much of a boat, and they'd make a fit pair, for he wasn't much of a small-boat sailor. His seamanship had been picked up on freighters and one tanker, and his time in sail was limited to a few weeks where somebody else was giving orders. He'd done one job of single handing with a small boat and had been shot with luck. On one of the most dangerous seas he had experienced nothing but flying-fish weather all the way.

Still, it was only eighty miles to Woodlark, and if the weather remained unchanged, he'd be all right. If—

The boy was there. "Three of them," he said, "three mans—very bad mans." And then he added, "They come tonight, I think."

So how much of a choice did he have? He left at dark or before dark, or he stayed and took a chance on being murdered or killing somebody. Anyway, the sea was quiet, only a little breeze running, and eighty miles was nothing.

The best way to cope with trouble was to avoid it, to stay away from where trouble was apt to be.

The only thing between where he was and Woodlark were the Alcesters. He had sailed by them before and would know them when he saw them.

He glanced down at the boy. "I'll leave the boat on Woodlark."

The boy shrugged. "Wherever."

He had shoved off at sundown with a good breeze blowing, and even with his caution he made good time, or what was good time for him. He had the Alcesters abeam before daybreak, but there was a boat behind him that was coming on fast. His silhouette was low, so he lowered the sail a little to provide even less and gradually eased the helm over and slid in behind one of the Alcesters.

It was nearing daylight, but suddenly it began to grow darker, and the wind began blowing in little puffs, and there was a brief spatter of rain. He was running before the wind when the storm came, and from that time on it was sheer panic. On the second or third day—he could not remember which—he piled up on the reef, a big wave carrying the boat over into the lagoon, ripping the hull open somewhere en route.

When daylight came again, the storm was blowing itself out; the boat was gone but for a length of broken mast and a piece of the forward section that contained a spare sail, some line, and some odds and ends of canned goods. And the gold.

He had saved the gold.

Dawn was a sickly thing on that first morning, with the northern sun remote behind gray clouds. He made his way along the reef, avoiding the lacerating edges of the coral until he reached the bar.

The old freighter, one mast still standing and a gaping hole in her hull, was high and dry on the sandbar. A flock of gulls rose screaming into the air as he approached, and he walked over the soft sand into the hole.

The deck above him was solid and strong. Far down there was a hatch, its cover stove in, which allowed a little light at the forward end. Here all was secure. Sand had washed in, making a hard-packed floor. Dugan put down a tin of biscuits and the few cans he had brought along and went back outside.

It was just one hundred and fifty steps to the water of the lagoon and the hollow in the reef where rain had collected in the natural cistern. The hollow in the reef was just three feet deep and about the size of a washtub. It was half full, and the water, although fresh, was warm.

For the moment he had food, shelter, and water.

Gathering driftwood, of which there was a good bit, he built a shade over the cistern that would prevent a too rapid evaporation but could be removed when it rained.

There would be fish, shellfish and crabs. For a time there might be eggs, and the first thing he must do would be to cover the reef, as much of it as he could reach, and see what he could find that was useful. Then he must get a fragment of that torn canvas and make a pennant to fly from the mast of the wrecked ship.

The work kept him busy. Scrambling over the reef,

careful not to slip into a hole or break an ankle on the rough, often slippery rock, he gathered driftwood. Slowly the several piles grew.

At night he sat beside his fire in the hulk and ate fish and a biscuit.

After a while he lost all awareness of the sea. It was there, all around him, and it was empty. Occasionally, when his eyes strayed that way, he saw distant smoke. He rarely looked at the sack of gold.

For the first time he deliberately faced his situation. From his pocket he took the worn chart, but he did not need it to face the fact. The reef was a lonely, isolated spot in the Coral Sea, in an area where ships came but rarely. Aside from the sandbar itself there was only the ruffled water and a few black stumps of coral rising above it.

This was no place for a man. It was a place for the wind and the gulls, yet there was a little water, there was a little food, and while a man lived, there was always a chance. It was then that he looked up and saw the schooner.

It was tacking, taking a course that would bring it closer to the reef. He shouted and waved a hand, and somebody waved back. He turned and walked toward the wreck.

When the dinghy came in close to pick him up, he waded out and lifted his bag of gold into the boat. Then he climbed in. There were two men in the dinghy, and they stared at him. "My—my water—it was about gone. You came just in time."

The men stared at the sack, then at him. The place where the sack rested against the thwart had dented the sack. Only sand or flour or something of the kind would make such an impression. And the sack had been heavy. He couldn't say it was shells or clothing. They'd know he lied.

Yet it was not until he came alongside the schooner

that he realized how much trouble he had bought for himself. He glanced at the schooner's name and felt a chill.

The *Dancing Kate*.

Bloody Jack Randall's schooner. Of course, he was never called Bloody Jack to his face, but behind his back they knew him by that name. He had killed a man in a saloon brawl at Port Moresby. There'd been a man shot in Kalgoorlie, but insufficient evidence released Randall. He was reported to have broken jail in New Caledonia after killing a guard.

After he was aboard, it was Randall's mate, a lean, wiry man with haggard features, who kicked the sack. "Hey? What you got in there? It looks mighty heavy."

"Gold."

It was a sullen, heavy day with thick clouds overhead and a small sea running. Kahler's eyes went to the sack again. "Gold?" He was incredulous.

"Yes." He slid his knife into his hand, point toward them, cutting edge uppermost. "This weighs about a pound. I measured the weight by this, and it is more than they thought."

"They?"

"A man in Misima asked me to deliver it to his granddaughter in Sydney."

"What kind of a damned fool would do that?" Kahler asked.

"A man who knew who he could trust." He glanced at Randall. "Where you bound?"

Randall hesitated. "East," he said finally, "We been scouting around."

"How about Woodlark? I'll pay my passage."

"All right." Randall walked forward and gave the change of course to the Bugi seaman. There were four of the Bugis, some of the best sailors among the islands; there was Randall himself, Kahler, and the big man who rowed the boat. That would be Sanguo Pete, a half-caste.

Taking his sack, he walked forward and sat down with his back against the foremast.

Kahler came forward. "We'll have chow pretty quick. One of those Bugis is a first-rate cook." He glanced down at him. "How'd you survive on that reef? You must be tough."

"I get along."

"By this time they probably figure you're dead," Kahler said.

"Maybe."

He knew what they were thinking. If something happened to him now, no one would know any better. Well, he promised himself, nothing was going to happen. He was going to meet Douglas at Woodlark.

When they went below to eat, he let them go first. He paused for a moment near one of the Bugi seamen. His Indonesian was just marketplace talk, but he could manage. He indicated the sack. "It is a trust," he said, "from a dying man. He has a granddaughter who needs this." He gestured toward the reef. "The sea was kind," he said.

"You are favored," the Bugi replied.

"If there is trouble—?"

"We are men of the sea. The troubles of white men are the troubles of white men."

He went below. There was a plate of food at the empty place. Randall had not begun to eat. Coolly, before Randall could object, he switched plates with him.

"What's the matter?" Randall demanded. "Don't you trust me?"

"I trust nobody," he said. "Nobody, Mr. Randall."

"You know me?"

"I know you. Douglas told me about you."

They exchanged glances. "Douglas? What do you know about him?"

"I'm his second mate. I'm joining him at Woodlark.

Then we'll arrange to get this"—he kicked the sack—
"to that girl in Sydney."

"Why bother?" Kahler said. "A man could have
himself a time with that much gold."

"And it will buy that girl an education."

"Hell! She'll get along—somehow."

The food was good, and when supper was over, he
took his gold and went on deck. Randall was a very
tough, dangerous man. So were the others, and it was
three to one. He could have used Douglas or Hilde-
brand. Or Charlie—most of all, Charlie.

The sails hung slack, and the moon was out. There
was a Bugi at the wheel, another on lookout in the
bow. These were tricky, dangerous waters, much of
them unsurveyed. He settled himself against the mainmast for a night of watching.

The storm that had wrecked his boat had blown him
east, far off his course. It could be no less than a
hundred miles to Misima and probably a good bit
more.

The hours dragged. A light breeze had come up, and
the vessel was moving along at a good clip. The moon
climbed to the zenith, then slid down toward the ocean
again. He dozed. The warmth of the night, the easy
motion of the schooner, the food in his stomach,
helped to make him sleepy. But he stayed awake.
They, of course, could sleep by turns.

At one time or another there had been a good bit of
talk about Randall, Sanguo Pete, and Kahler. They
had a hand in more than one bit of doubtful activity.
He was half asleep when they suddenly closed in on
him. At one moment he had been thinking of what
he'd heard about them, and he must have dozed off,
for they closed in quickly and silently. Some faint
sound of bare feet on the deck must have warned him
even as they reached for him.

He saw the gleam of starlight on steel, and he ripped

up with his own knife. The man pulled back sharply, and his blade sliced open a shirt, and the tip of his knife drew a red line from navel to chin, nicking the chin hard as the man drew back.

Then he was on his feet. Somebody struck at him with a marlin spike, and he parried the blow with his blade and lunged. The knife went in; he felt his knuckles come up hard against warm flesh, and he withdrew the knife as he dodged a blow at his head.

The light was bad, for them as well as for him, and one might have been more successful than three; as it was, they got in each other's way in the darkness. The man he had stabbed had gone to the deck, and in trying to crawl away, tripped up another.

He had his gun but dared not reach for it. It meant shifting the knife, and even a moment off guard would be all they would need.

One feinted a rush. The man on the deck was on his feet, and they were spreading out. Suddenly they closed in. The half light was confusing, and as he moved to get closer to one man, he heard another coming in from behind. He tried to make a quick half turn, but a belaying pin caught him alongside the skull. Only a glancing blow, but it dazed him, and he fell against the rail. He took a cut at the nearest man, missed but ripped into another. How seriously, he did not know. Then another blow caught him, and he felt himself falling.

He hit the water and went down. When he came up, the boat was swinging. The Bugi at the wheel was swinging the bow around. As the hull went away from him, the bow came to him, and there were the stays. He grabbed hold and pulled himself up to the bowsprit.

For a moment he hung there, gasping for breath. He could see them peering over the rail.

"Did you get him, cap?"

"Get him? You damned right I did! He's a goner."
He turned then. "You cut bad, Pete?"

"I'm bleedin'. I got to get the blood stopped."

"He got me, too," Kahler said. "You sure we got
him?"

Randall waved at the dark water. "You don't see
him, do you? We got him, all right."

After a moment they went below, and the tall yellow
seaman at the wheel glanced at the foremast against
the sky, lined it up with his star. His expression did not
change when he saw Dugan come over the bow and
crouch low.

There was no sound but the rustle of bow wash, the
creak of rigging, and a murmur of voices aft. He
moved aft, exchanging one glance with the Bugi, and
when he was close enough, he said, "Thanks." Not
knowing if the man understood, he repeated, *"Terima
kasi."*

He knew the Bugi had deliberately put the rigging
below the bowsprit in his way. The wonder was that
even with the distraction of the fighting Randall had
not noticed it.

His gun was still in the side pocket of his pants, and
he took it out, struggling a bit to do so, as the dungarees were a tight fit. He put the gun in his hip pocket
where it was easier of access. He did not want to use a
gun, and neither did they. Bullet scars were not easy to
disguise and hard to explain when found on rails or
deck houses.

Sanguo Pete loomed in the companionway and stood
blinking at the change from light to darkness. There
was a gash on his cheekbone that had been taped shut,
and there was a large mouse over one eye. He hitched
up his dungarees and started forward, a gun strapped
to his hips. He had taken but two steps when he saw
Dugan crouched close to the rail.

Pete broke his paralysis and yelled, then grabbed for
his gun. It was too late to think about the future

questions. As Pete's hand closed on the butt, Dugan shot him.

Randall loomed in the companionway, but all he saw was the wink of fire from Dugan's gun. He fell forward, half on deck.

Pete lay in the scuppers, his big body rolling slightly with the schooner.

The Bugi looked at Dugan and said, "No good mans."

"No good," Dugan agreed.

One by one he tilted them over the side and gave them to the sea.

"My ship is waiting at Woodlark Island," Dugan said.

The Bugi glanced at him. "Is Cap'n Douglas ship. I know." Suddenly he smiled. "I have two brother on your ship—long time now."

"Two brothers? Well, I'll be damned!"

Kahler was lying on the bunk when he went below. His body had been bandaged, but he had lost blood.

"We're going to Woodlark," Dugan said. "If you behave yourself, you might make it."

Kahler closed his eyes, and Dugan lay down on the other bunk and looked up at the deck overhead. The day after tomorrow—

It would be good to be back aboard, lying in his own bunk. He remembered the brief note in the Pilot Book for the area.

This coral reef, discovered in 1825, lies about 82 miles east-northeast of Rossel Island. The reef is 18 miles in length, in a northeast and southwest direction. The greatest breadth is 3 miles, but in some places it is not more than a mile wide. At the northeastern end of the reef there are some rocks 6 feet high. No anchorage is available off the reef.

Wreck. The wreck of a large iron vessel above

water lies (1880) on the middle of the southeastern side of the reef.

If they wanted to know any more, they could just ask him. He'd tell them.

GLORIOUS!

In 1893 and again in 1909 Riffian tribesmen attacked Spanish settlements in Spanish Morocco. Finally, in 1921, this became an all-out war that resulted in a series of defeats for the Spanish. In the battle at Anual an army of twenty thousand men was thoroughly defeated by the Riffs under Abd-el-Krim, and twelve thousand were slain. Fighting continued for five years, and the Spanish Foreign Legion was in the thick of it.

Supply lines to many scattered outposts were cut or severely hampered by mud caused by torrential rains that made travel difficult to impossible. Much bravery was exhibited by officers and men, but among their superiors there was often total incompetence.

Chentafa was destroyed, and Seriya held off repeated attacks for seventy-odd days before the post was wiped out.

Abd-el-Krim was a competent commander and an able tactician, as were several of his subordinates. He was only defeated when the French came into the fight, and he was exiled to the isle of Reunion in the Indian Ocean, installed on a country estate, and provided with a considerable pension.

The Riffs are a Berber people, excellent rifle shots, and first-class fighting men. From about 15,000 B.C. Berbers occupied just about all of North Africa, including the Sahara. The veiled Tuareg, once considered the fiercest of desert raiders, were Berbers. Among the Riffs the per-

centage of red-heads is about the same as can
be found in Scotland or Ireland.

In my story I have used the terms Moor and
Riff interchangeably. Correctly speaking, a Moor
is of the Arab race but born in Morocco. As a
matter of fact a large percentage are of mixed
Arab and Berber blood. The Riffs are so called
because of their residence in the Riff Hills, a part
of the Atlas Mountains, a lovely but rugged
country cloaked in pine and cedar.

THE FOUR MEN crouched together in the narrow shadow of the parapet. The sun was setting slowly behind a curtain of greasy cloud, and the air, as always at twilight, was very clear and still. A hundred and fifty yards away was the dirty gray earth where the Riffs were hidden. The declining sun threw long fingers of queer, brassy light across the rise of the hill behind them.

On their left the trench was blown away by artillery fire; here and there a foot or a shoulder showed above the dirt thrown up by explosions. They had marched, eaten, and fought beside those men, dead now.

"Better keep your head away from that opening, kid, or you'll get it blown away."

Dugan pulled his head back, and almost on the instant a spout of sand leaped from the sandbag and splattered over his face.

Slim smiled wryly, and the Biscayan looked up from the knife he was sharpening. He was always sharpening his knife and kept it with a razor edge. Short, thick-bodied, he had a square-jawed, pockmarked face and small eyes. Dugan was glad they were fighting on the same side.

"You got anything to eat?" Slim asked suddenly, looking over at Dugan.

"Nothing. I ate my last biscuit before that last attack," he said. "I could have eaten forty."

"You?" Slim looked at the Irishman.

Jerry shrugged. "I ate mine so long ago I've forgotten."

He was bandaging his foot with a soiled piece of his shirt. A bullet had clipped the butt of his heel the day before, making a nasty wound.

Somewhere down the broken line of trenches there was a brief volley followed by several spaced rifle shots, then another brief spatter of firing.

Slim was wiping the dust from his rifle, testing the action. Then he reloaded, taking his time. "They're tough," he said, "real tough."

"I figured they'd be A-rabs or black," Jerry said, "and they ain't either one."

"North Africa was never black," Dugan said. "Nearly all the country north of the Niger is Berber country, and Berbers are white. These Riffs—there's as many redheaded ones as in Scotland."

"I was in Carthage once," Slim said. "It's all busted up—ruins."

"They were Semitic," Dugan said. "Phoenicians originally."

"How you know so much about it?" Slim asked.

"There was a book somebody left in the barracks all about this country and the Sahara."

"You can have it," Jerry said. "This country, I mean."

"Book belonged to that colonel—the fat one." Dugan moved a small stone, settled himself more comfortably. "He let it lay one time, and somebody swiped it."

"Hey!" Jerry sat up suddenly. He held the bandage tight to survey the job he was doing, then continued with it. "That reminds me. I know where there's some wine."

Slim turned his long neck. "Some *what?*"

He looked gaunt and gloomy in his dirty, ill-fitting uniform. One shoulder was stained with blood, and the threads had begun to ravel around a bullet hole. He had been hit nine times since the fighting began, but mostly they were scratches. He'd lost one shoe, and the foot was wrapped in canvas. It was a swell war.

Jerry continued to wrap his foot, and nobody said anything. Dugan watched him, thinking of the wine. Then he looked across at the neat row of men lying side by side near the far parapet. As he looked, a bullet struck one of them, and the body jerked stiffly. It did not matter. They were all dead.

"Over there in the cellar," Jerry said. He nodded his head to indicate a squat gray stone building on the peak of a conical hill about a quarter of a mile off. "The colonel found a cellar the monks had. He brought his own wine with him and a lot of canned meat and cheese. He stored it in that cellar—just like in an icebox. I helped pack some of it in not over two weeks ago. He kept me on patrol duty three days extra just for breaking a bottle. He brought in a lot of grub, too."

The Biscayan glanced up, mumbling something in Spanish. He pulled a hair from his head and tested the edge of the blade, showing his teeth when the hair cut neatly.

"What's he say?"

"He says it may still be there." Jerry shifted his rifle and glanced speculatively at the low hill. "Shall we have a look?"

"They'd blow our heads off before we could get there," Slim protested, "night or no night."

"Look," Jerry said, "we're liable to get it, anyway. This is going to be like Anual, where they wiped them all out. Look how long we've been here and no relief. I think they've written us off."

"It's been seventy-five days," Dugan agreed.

"Look what happened at Chentafa. The officer in command saw they'd had it and set fire to the post; then he died with his men."

"That's more than these will do."

"Hell," Jerry said, "I think they're already dead. I haven't seen an officer in a week. Only that corporal."

"They pick them off first. Those Moors can shoot." Slim looked at Dugan. "How'd you get into this outfit, anyway?"

"My ship was in Barcelona. I came ashore and was shanghaied. I mean an army patrol just gathered in a lot of us, and when I said I was an American citizen, they just paid no attention."

"Did you get any training?"

"A week. That was it. They asked me if I'd ever fired a gun, and like a damned fool I told them I had. Hell, I grew up with a gun. I was twelve years old before I found out it wasn't part of me. So here I am."

"They wanted men, and they didn't care where or how they got them. Me, I've no excuse," Slim said, "I joined the Spanish Foreign Legion on my own. I was broke, hungry, and in a different country. It looked like an easy way out."

Far off to the left there was an outburst of firing, then silence.

"What happened to the colonel? The fat one who had all that wine brought in?"

"Killed himself. Look, they tell me there's a general for every twenty-five men in this army. This colonel had connections. They told him spend a month over there and we'll promote you to general, so he came, and then we got pinned down, and he couldn't get out. From Tetuan to Chaouen there's a whole line of posts like this one here at Seriya. There's no way to get supplies, no way to communicate."

The talk died away. It was very hot even though the sun was setting.

A big Russian came up and joined them. He looked

like a big schoolboy with his close-cropped yellow hair and his pink cheeks. "They come," he said.

There was a crackle of shots, and the four climbed to their feet. Dugan lurched from weariness, caught himself, and faced about. The Russian was already firing.

A long line of Moors was coming down the opposite slope, their advance covered by a barrage of machine-gun fire from the trenches farther up the hill. Here and there a captured field gun boomed. Dugan broke open a box of cartridges and laid them out on a sandbag close at hand. Slowly and methodically, making each shot count, he began to fire.

The Biscayan was muttering curses and firing rapidly. He did not like long-range fighting. Jerry leaned against the sandbags, resting his forehead on one. Dugan could see a trickle of sweat cutting a trail through the dust.

Somewhere down the parapet one of their own machine guns opened up, the gray and white line before them melted like wax, and the attack broke. Slim grounded his rifle butt and leaned against the sandbags, fumbling for a cigarette. His narrow, cadaverous features looked yellow in the pale light. He looked around at Dugan. "How d'you like it, kid? Had enough?"

Dugan shrugged and reloaded his rifle, then stuffed his pockets with cartridges. The powder smoke made his head ache, or maybe it was hunger and the sound of guns. His cheek was swollen from the rifle stock, and his gums were sore and swollen. All of them were indescribably dirty. For seventy-five days they had held the outpost against a steady, unrelenting, consistent, energy-draining attack that seemed to take no thought of men lost. Their food was gone; only a little of the brackish water remained, and there would be no relief.

"They've written us off," Slim said. "We're dead." He was hollow eyed and sagging, yet he was still a fighting man. He looked at Jerry. "How about that wine?"

"Let's go get it. There's a machine gun there, too, and enough ammo to fight the battle of the Marne."

"Does the sergeant major know?"

"He did." Jerry indicated the line of dead bodies. "He's over there."

"Who's in command?" Dugan asked.

"Maybe nobody. The lieutenant was killed several days ago, shot from behind. He was a fool to hit that Turk. He slugged one guy too many."

The sun was gone, and darkness was falling over the low hills. There was no movement in the trenches across the way. The Russian stood up, then sat down abruptly, his throat shot away. He started to rise again, then just sat back down and slowly rolled over.

Slim picked him up as though he were a child and carried him to the line of bodies, placing him gently on the ground. Then he unbuckled his cartridge pouches and hung them around his own waist. Dugan looked through an opening in the sandbagged parapet at the broad shoulders of shadow along the slope. A dead Moor hung head down over the barbed wire about fifty feet away, and a slight breeze made his burnoose swell.

When it was dark, the corporal came along the trench. He looked old. His thin, haggard face was expressionless. He said what they all knew.

"There won't be any relief. I think everything behind us is wiped out, too. We wouldn't stand a chance in trying to get away. They're out there waiting, hoping we try it.

"There'll be at least one night attack, but with daybreak they'll come. There's thirty-eight of us left. Fire as long as you can, and when they get through the wire, it's every man for himself."

He looked around vacantly, then started back up the line. His shoes were broken, and one leg was bandaged. He looked tired. He stopped suddenly, looking back. "If any of you have the guts to try it, go ahead." He looked from Jerry to Slim, then at Dugan. "We're through."

Slim walked over to the dead officer and took his automatic, then the cartridges for it. He took some money, too, then dropped it into the sand. Having a second thought, he picked it up.

"If a man could get away," he said, looking over at Dugan, "this would pay a boatman. Gibraltar—that would be the place."

Dugan sat down, his back to the parapet. He glanced along the trench. Far down he could see movement.

Thirty-eight left! There had been 374 when they occupied the post. He tilted his head back and looked at the stars. They had looked the same way at home. How long ago was that?

Jerry got up. He glanced at Slim, and the Texan shrugged. "Let's go," he said. And they went.

Jerry pointed. "We'll go down that shallow place, and there's a ditch. Follow that to the right and it takes you right up to the building. If we get into that ditch, we've got it made."

There was no moon, but the stars were bright. The rear parapet had been partly knocked down by the explosion of a shell. They went over fast, Jerry first, then Dugan. Flat on their faces, they wormed across the dark ground, moving fast but silently. The ground was still hot. In the darkness his hand touched something warm. It was a gun, an automatic. He thought of Slim and felt suddenly sick; then he remembered the sergeant who had been killed out here a few days before. He took the gun but turned at right angles. The Biscayan was close beside him, his knife in his teeth, his rifle lying across his forearms.

Dugan heard a slight movement and looked up suddenly into the eyes of a Moor. For a split second they both stared, and then Dugan jerked his rifle forward, and the muzzle struck the Moor right below the eye. The Moor rolled back and then came up, very fast, with a knife. Dugan kicked him on the kneecap, then hit him with the butt and followed with the barrel. He went down, but another loomed up.

There was a scream as the Biscayan ripped one up, and then Slim broke into the fight with an automatic. Then there was a roar of shots from all along the parapet. It was the expected night attack, sooner than believed and almost successful.

Dugan came up running, saw a Moor loom up before him, and shot without lifting the rifle above his belt line. The Moor spun out of the way and fell, and Dugan fell into the ditch just one jump ahead of the Biscayan. Then Slim and Jerry joined them. Jerry was carrying three rifles and a bandoleer of cartridges.

They went along the ditch at a stumbling run. Dugan slipped once and almost fell, but when he straightened up, the stone house was looming above them. Jerry led them to the trap door at the end of the ditch.

The room was empty except for a desk and a couple of chairs. One chair was tipped on its side, and there were papers scattered about. The room had a musty smell, as the door and windows were heavily shuttered and barred. Both openings could be covered by rifles from the trenches below, and as the position was not a good one, the Moors had not taken it.

Jerry dragged the heavy desk aside and struck a match to find the iron ring concealed in a crack. With a heave he opened the cellar. In the flare of the match Dugan saw that Jerry's scalp was deeply lacerated and dried blood matted his hair on one side.

Slim slid into the hole and a moment later was

handing up bottles. Then he sent up a magnum of champagne, and the Biscayan came up with some canned fruit and cheese.

"This guy had a taste for knickknacks," Slim said. "There's everything down here that you could get into a can."

"He took three hot ones right through the belly on the first day," Jerry said. "He was scared and crying like a baby. I don't believe he'd ever done a day's duty in his life."

Dugan took a bottle of Chateau Margaux and a can of the cheese. The wine tasted good. After a bit he crawled into a corner, made a pillow of some cartridge pouches, and went to sleep. When he awakened, light was filtering into the room from around the shutters. Jerry was sitting wide legged near the cellar door, and he was drunk. Slim was at the desk.

"Kid," Slim said, "come here."

He had a map laid out. "See? If you get the chance, take the ditch to here, then down along that dry creek. It's not far to the coast, and most of those boat guys will give you a lift for money. You got any money?"

"About twenty bucks. I've been hiding it in case."

"Here." Slim took the money he'd taken from the dead officer. "You take this."

"What about you?"

"I ain't goin' to make it, kid. I got a hunch. If I do, we'll go together. If you board that boat, they may take your rifle, but you keep your sidearm, you hear? Keep it hidden. You may need it before you get across."

He turned to look at Dugan. "How old are you, kid?"

"Twenty-two," Dugan said, and he lied. He was just past sixteen.

"You look younger. Anyway, go through their pockets, whoever's dead. They won't mind, and you'll need whatever there is.

"Don't go near the army or a big town. Head for the seacoast and stay out of sight. Anybody you meet out here will try to stop you. Don't let it happen. You get away—you hear?"

Jerry lifted the bottle in a toast. "Tomorrow we die!" he said.

"Today, you mean," Slim said.

The Biscayan came up from the cellar with a machine gun. It was brand-spanking-new. He went down again and came up with several belts of ammo, then a box of them. He set the machine gun up at a shuttered window and fed a belt into it.

Dugan looked at the automatic he had picked up. It was in good shape. He found another in the cellar and several spare clips. He loaded them.

Scattered shooting broke into a steady roar. A shell exploded not too far away.

Slim had found two Spanish versions of the Colt pistols and loaded them. He strapped them on, pleased. "You know what I'm going to do? I'm going to get good and drunk, and then I'm going to open that door and show them how we do it down in Texas!"

He emptied half a bottle of the wine and looked at Dugan. "You ever been in Texas, kid?"

"I worked on a ranch there—in the Panhandle."

"I grew up on a ranch," Slim said. "Rode for a couple of outfits in New Mexico before I started out to see the world. I knew this would happen sometime. Just never figured it would be here, in a place like this."

He picked up the bottle of wine and looked at it. "What I need is some tequila. This here is a she-male's drink! Or some bourbon an' branch water."

Dugan took his rifle and walked to the window. He

helped the Biscayan move the machine gun to a more advantageous position, a little closer, a little more to the left. He checked his rifle again and loaded two more and stood them close by. From a crack in the shutters he studied the route he might get a chance to take. It must be done before the whole country was overrun by the Moors.

Suddenly Jerry moved, the dried blood still caked in his stubble of beard. He crawled on hands and knees to the edge of the trapdoor from the ditch. Then he stopped, breathing hoarsely, waiting.

Dugan had heard nothing above the occasional rattle of distant rifle fire as the Riffs began to mop up. Suddenly the trapdoor began to lift, very cautiously, then with more confidence. When it had lifted about a foot, a big Riff thrust his head up and stared into the room. All the occupants were out of his immediate range, and he lifted his head higher, peering into the semidarkness. In that instant Jerry swung the empty magnum. The solid *bop* of the blow was loud in the room, and the man vanished, the door falling into place. Jerry jerked it open, slammed it back, and leaped down into the hole. There was a brief scuffle, and then Jerry came back through the trap door, carrying a new rifle and a bandoleer.

Now the crescendo of firing had lifted to a loud and continuous roar, and Slim started to sing. In the tight stone room his voice boomed loudly.

Glorious! Glorious!
One keg o' beer for the four of us!
Glory be to heaven that there isn't
ten or 'leven,
For the four of us can drink it all alone!

The Biscayan took down the bar and threw the shutters wide. Below them and away across the tawny hill the Riffian trench was suddenly vomiting up a long line of men. From behind the parapet before them a scattering fire threw a pitiful challenge at the charging line.

Dugan wiped the sweat from his eyebrows and leaned against the edge of the window. He was sagging with incredible exhaustion, and his body stank from the unwashed weeks, the sweat and the dirt. He lifted the rifle and held it against his swollen cheek and began to fire.

Behind him Jerry and Slim were singing "Casey Jones." Dugan looked down at the Biscayan, a solid chunk of man who lived to fight. Hunched behind the machine gun, he waited, watching the line as an angler watches a big fish approaching the hook.

Suddenly the firing stopped, waiting for a killing volley at close quarters.

Dugan had stopped, too. One man, a tall Moor on a fine-looking horse, had ridden out on a point a good six hundred yards away, watching the attack. He stood in his stirrups, lifting a hand to shout a command, unheard at the distance. For what seemed a long minute Dugan held his aim, then squeezed off the shot, and the man stood tall in his stirrups, then fell from the saddle to the dust and lay there. Then the Biscayan opened fire.

Dugan looked down at him, aware for the first time that the Biscayan was drunk. The gray line melted before him, and the Biscayan lifted the bottle for another drink.

The unexpected fire from the stone house, cutting a wide swath in their ranks, paralyzed the attack. Then a bunch of the Riffs broke away from the main attack and started toward the stone house. Jerry was up, firing slowly, methodically. Suddenly the machine gun swung, fired three short bursts, and the bunch of attackers melted away. From behind the parapet came a wavering cheer. Dugan winced at the few voices. So many were gone!

Dugan squinted his eyes against the sun, remembering the line of silent men beside the parapet and the big Russian with the schoolboy pink in his cheeks.

The Biscayan lifted his bottle to drink, and it shattered in his hand, spilling wine over him. With a lurid burst of Spanish he dropped the neck of the bottle and reached for another. And he had never been a drinking man.

Slim sat on the floor, muttering. "I'm goin' to get damn good an' drunk an' go out there and show 'em how we do it down in Texas."

He started to rise and sat down hard, a long red furrow along his jaw. He swore in a dull, monotonous voice.

Dugan saw the line of Moors sweep forward and across the parapet. There was scattered shooting, some rising dust, then silence. He blinked, feeling a lump in his throat. He had known few of them, for they had been together too short a time. Only weeks had passed since he lay in his bunk aboard ship, feeling the gentle roll as it steamed west from Port Said.

The sunlight was bright and clear. Outside, except for the scattered bodies of the slain, all was quiet and peaceful under the morning sun. Dugan looked across the valley, thinking of what he would do. There was little time. Perhaps time had already run out.

The afternoon was waning before they attacked again. This time they were careful, taking advantage of the slight roll of the hill to get closer. The last hundred yards was in the open, and they seemed unaware of the ditch, which would be hidden from them until they were almost fallen into it.

Dugan's face was swollen and sore from the kick of the rifle. He was hot and tired, and he switched rifles again.

A single shot sounded, lonely against the hills, and something gasped beside him. He turned to see Jerry fall across the sill. Before he could pull him back, three more bullets chugged into his body.

"Kid," Slim said, "you better go. It's time."

He took the bar down from the door and looked down the sunlit hill. A knot of Moors was coming toward him, good men, fighting men, dangerous men. Slim stepped out with a pistol in each hand and started down toward them.

He was drunk. Magnificently, roaring drunk, and he had a pistol in either hand. "I'm a-goin' to show them how we do it down in Texas!" He opened fire, then his body jerked, and he went to his knees.

Dugan snapped a quick shot at a Moor running up with a rifle ready to fire, and then Slim got up. He had lost one gun, but he started to fire from waist level. His whole left side was bloody.

Dugan turned to yell at the Biscayan, but the man was slumped across his machine gun. He had been shot between the eyes.

Dugan pushed him away from the gun and swung it toward the front of the house. In the distance, against the pale-blue sky, above the heat waves dancing, a vulture swung in slow circles against the sky. Slim was down, all sprawled out, and the enemy was closing in.

He pointed the gun toward them and opened up, singing in a hoarse, toneless voice.

> Glorious! Glorious!
> One keg o' beer for the four of us!
> Glory be to heaven that there isn't
> ten or 'leven,
> For the four of us can drink it all alone!

His belt went empty, and the hill was bare of all but the bodies. He got up and closed the heavy plank door.

He caught up a bandoleer and another pistol. Then he dropped through the trapdoor.

All was still. He stepped over the dead Moor and went out into the shadowed stillness of the ditch.

And then he began to run.

DEAD-END DRIFT

Most of these stories were written in retrospect, when the events that led to them were already far behind. Fortunately I never experienced what happened in this story but thought of it from time to time. Such things were not much talked about, but I worked with miners who had survived them.

I never worked in a coal mine, only in hard-rock mines in the West, in one copper mine, in several silver, lead, and zinc or gold mines. Often several minerals were found in the same mine. In some silver or copper mines enough gold is found to pay the expense of mining. I was never an expert miner, although I've worked with a stopper. Usually they had me tramming or on the business end of a muck stick (shovel), and at the latter, I always felt I need take second place to no man. (I was probably wrong.) I was also a better than fair hand with a double jack (sledgehammer).

In the larger mines we usually came out to the station to eat our lunches and to wait when the shift was over to let the miners count their shots. Those were great times for me, as many of the older miners had worked the boom camps such as Tonopah, Goldfield, Rawhide, Cripple Creek, Leadville, Central City, and Virginia City. Resting time was also a time when they told stories or talked about characters they had known such as Ten-Day Murphy, Slasher Harrington, and Shorty Harris.

Shorty was always a favorite character of mine

because of the rare sort of character he was. He made big mining discoveries but never cashed in on any of them, but at the end he was buried standing up at the bottom of Death Valley, and he would have liked that.

Boxing had always been a major interest of mine, and we had a tough old Irish miner there who had boxed a four-round exhibition with John L. Sullivan and several who had known Jack Dempsey when he was a saloon bouncer or worked in the mines. They had also seen him fight. And Malloy, Johnny Sudenberg, and some of the early fighters.

I met Jack briefly once when eating lunch in his New York restaurant but never told him I'd fought in some of the same places or worked in the same mining camps.

There were miners there who had seen Joe Gans fight Battling Nelson for the world's lightweight title in Goldfield. Joe Gans won on a foul in forty-two rounds.

There are still stories from those days that I must write and will write. There are ghost stories, fight stories, and even the story of a man who was going to raise the dead. He even invited everybody to come and see him do it.

THE TRICKLE OF SAND ceased, and there was silence. Then a small rock dropped from overhead into the rubble beneath, and the flat finality of the sound put a period to the moment.

There was a heavy odor of dust, and one of the men coughed, the dry, hacking cough of miner's consumption. Silence hung heavily in the thick, dead air.

"Better sit still." Bert's voice was quiet and unexcited. "I'll make a light." They waited, listening to the miner fumbling with his hand lamp. "We might dislodge something," he added, "and start it again."

They heard his palm strike the lamp, and he struck several times before the flint gave off the spark to light the flame. An arrow of flame leaped from the burner. The sudden change from the impenetrable darkness at the end of the tunnel to the bright glare of the miner's lamp left them blinking. They sat very still, looking slowly around, careful to disturb nothing. The suddenness of the disaster had stunned them into quiet acceptance.

Frank's breathing made a hoarse, ugly sound, and when their eyes found him, they could see the dark, spreading stain on his shirt front and the misshapen look of his broken body. He was a powerful man, with blond, curly hair above a square, hard face. There was blood on the rocks near him and blood on the jagged rock he had rolled from his body after the cave-in.

There was a trickle of blood across Bert's face from a scalp wound but no other injuries to anyone. Their eyes evaded the wall of fallen rock across the drift, their minds filled with awareness.

"Hurt bad?" Bert said to Frank. "Looks like the big one hit you."

"Yeah," Frank's voice was low. "Feels like I'm stove up inside."

"Better leave him alone," Joe said. "The bleeding seems to be letting up, and there's nothing we can do."

Frank stared down at his body curiously. "I guess I'm hurt bad."

He turned his head deliberately and stared at the muck pile. The cave-in had left a slanting pile of broken rock that reached toward them along the drift, cutting them off completely from the outside world, from light and air. Behind them was the face of the drift where Rody had been drilling. From the face of the drift to the muck pile was a matter of a few feet. Frank touched his dry lips with his tongue, remembering what lay beyond the cave-in.

It could scarcely have been the tunnel alone. Beyond it was the Big Stope. He reached over and turned out the light. The flame winked, and darkness was upon them.

"What's the idea?" Joe demanded.

"Air," Frank said. "There's four of us, and there isn't going to be enough air. We may be some time in getting out."

"If we get out," Joe said.

Rody shifted his weight on the rock slab where he was sitting, and they heard the rasp of the coarse denim. "How far do you reckon she caved, Frank?"

"I don't know." Then he said what they all feared. "Maybe the Big Stope went."

"If it did," Rody commented, "we might as well fold our cards and toss in our hands. Nobody can open that stope before the air gives out. There's not much air in here for four men."

"I warned Tom about that stope," Joe said. "He had no right to have men working in here. That stope was too big in the first place. Must be a hundred feet across and no pillars, and down below there was too much weight on the stulls. The posts were countersunk into the laggin' all of two inches, like a knife in butter."

"The point is," Frank said, "that we're here. No use talking about what should have been. If any part of the stope went, it all went. There's a hundred feet of tunnel to drive and timber, and workin' in loose muck isn't going to help."

No one spoke. In the utter blackness and stillness of the drift they waited. There was no light, no sound. All had been cut off from them. Joe wiped the sweat from his brow with the back of his hand.

The blackness of a mine, the complete darkness, had always bothered him. At night in the outer world, no matter how clouded the sky, there is always some light, and in time the eyes will adjust, and a man can see—a little, at any rate. Here there was no light, and a man was completely blind.

And there was no sound. Only two hundred feet to the surface, yet it might as well have been two thousand. Two hundred feet of rock between them and the light, and that was the shortest route. By the drift or tunnel it was a quarter of a mile to the shaft where the cage could take them to the surface.

Above them was the whole weight of the mountain, before them the solid wall where they had been drilling, behind them the mass of the cave-in, thousands of tons of broken rock and broken timbers.

On the surface there would be tense, frightened men, frightened not for themselves but for those entombed below—and they could not know that anyone was alive.

The skip would be coming down now, bringing men to attack that enormous slide. On top men would be girding for the struggle with the mountain. Around the collar of the shaft men and equipment would be gathered to be sent below. Near the warehouse men would be standing, and some women, tense and white, wondering about those below. And the men who were buried alive could only wait and hope.

"Got a chew, Bert?" Joe asked.

"Sure." Bert pushed his hand into the darkness, feeling for Joe's. Their hands were steady. Joe bit off a chew, then passed the plug back, their hands fumbling in the dark again.

"We ain't got a chance!" Rody exclaimed suddenly. "She might have caved clear to the station. Anyway, there's no way they can get through in time. We ain't got the air to last five hours even if they could make it that quick."

"Forget it," Joe said. "You wouldn't do nothing but blow your money on that frowzy blonde in Kingman if you got free."

"I was a sap for ever coming to work in this lousy hole," Rody grumbled. "I was a sap."

"Quit crabbing," Bert said mildly. "We're here now, and we've got to like it."

There was a long silence. Somewhere the mountain creaked, and there was a distant sound of more earth sliding.

"Say"—Frank's voice broke into the silence—"any of you guys work in Thirty-seven?"

"You mean that raise on the Three Hundred?" Bert asked. "Sure, I put in a couple of shifts there."

"Aren't we right over it now?"

"Huh?" Joe moved quickly. "How high up were they?"

"Better than ninety feet." Frank's tone was tight, strained. He held himself, afraid to breathe deep, afraid of the pain that would come. He was not sure what had happened to him. Part of his body was numb, but there was a growing pain in his belly as the shock wore off. He knew he was in deep trouble, and the chances of his getting out alive were small. He dreaded the thought of being moved, doubted if he would survive it.

"If that raise was up ninety feet"—Joe spoke slowly, every word standing alone—"then it ain't more than ten feet below us. If we could dig down—"

"Ten feet? In that kind of rock?" Rody sneered. "You couldn't dig that with a pick. Not in a week. Anyway, Thirty-seven ain't this far along. We're thirty yards beyond at least."

"No," Frank said, "I think we're right over it. Anyway, it's a chance. It's more than we've got now."

There was a long silence while they turned the idea over in their minds. Then Joe said, "Why a raise here? There's no ore body here. That's suppose to be further along."

"Air," Bert said. "They wanted some circulation."

He got up, and they heard him fumbling for a pick. They heard the metallic sound as it was dragged toward him over the rock. "Better move back against the muck pile," he said. "I'm digging."

"You're a sap," Rody said. "You've got no chance."

"Shut up!" Joe's tone was ugly. "If you ain't willing to try, you can go to hell. I want out of here."

"Who're you tellin' to shut up?" They heard Rody rise suddenly. "I ain't never had no use for you, you—"

"Rody!" Frank's tone was harsh. "I've got a pick handle, and I know where you are. You go back where you were and keep your mouth shut. This is a hell of a time to start something."

A light flared in Frank's hand, and he hitched himself a little higher to see better. "That's right, Bert. Start right there. Some of that top stuff will just flake off."

Sweat beaded his strained white face. One big hand clutched a pick handle. Slowly, as if he had difficulty in moving them, his eyes shifted from face to face. He stared at Rody the longest. Rody's stiff black hair curled back from a low forehead. He was almost as broad as Frank but thicker.

The sodden blows of the pick became the ticking clock of the passing time. It was a slow, measured beat, for the air was already thickening, and the blows pounded with the pulse of their blood. The flame of the carbide light ate into their small supply of air, burning steadily.

Bert stopped, mopping his face. "She's damn hard, Frank. It's going to take the point off this pick in a hurry."

"We've got four of them," Frank said. The whole front of him was one dark stain now. "I always carry a pick in a mine."

Bert swung again, and they watched as the point of the pick found a place and broke back a piece of the rock. The surface had been partly shattered by the explosions as the drift was pushed farther into the mountain. It would be harder as they got down farther.

Frank's big hands were relaxed and loose. He watched the swing of the pick, and when Joe got up to spell Bert, he asked him, "Anybody on top waitin' for you?"

"Uh-huh." Joe paused, pick in hand. "A girl."

Rody started to speak but caught Frank's eye and settled back, trying to move out of reach of the pick handle.

"My wife's up there," Bert said. "And I've got three kids." He took off his shirt and mopped his body with it.

"There's nobody waitin' for me," Frank said. "Nobody anywhere."

"What d'you suppose they're doing out there?" Bert said. "I'd give a lot to know."

"Depends on how far it caved." Joe leaned on the pick handle, gasping for breath. "Probably they are shoring her up with timbers around the station or at the opening into the Big Stope."

He returned to work. He swung the pick, and a fragment broke loose; a second time and another fragment. Bert sat with his elbows on his knees, head hanging, breathing heavily. Frank's head was tipped back against the rock, his white face glistening like wet marble in the faint light that reached him.

It was going to be a long job, a hard job, and the air was growing worse. Being active, they were using it more rapidly, but it was their only chance. Nobody could get through to them in time. As Joe worked, the sweat streamed from his body, running into his eyes and dripping from his chin. Slowly and methodically he swung the pick, deadened to everything but the shock of the blows. He no longer noticed what progress he made; he had become an automaton. Bert started up to relieve him, but Joe shook his head. He was started now, and it was like an infection in his blood. He needed the pick. He clung to it as to a life line.

At last he did give way to Bert. He dropped on the rocks, his chest heaving, fighting for air. He tried to keep from remembering Mary, but she was always with him, always just beyond the blows of his pick. Probably she did not yet know what had happened to them, what this sudden thing was that had come into their lives.

She would be at work now, and as the mine was forty miles from town, it might be hours before she knew of the cave-in and even longer before she knew who was trapped below. It would be her tragedy as well as his. Joe cursed. Tomorrow they would have gone to the doctor. He was reliable, Frank had told him, a good man and not a quack.

Big Frank knew about Mary. He knew that with every drive of the pick it would be a closer thing for her. There were but four of them here, underground, but outside were Mary and Bert's wife and kids. It would be a close thing, any way it was looked at. He, Joe, could take it. He had never done anything else, but Mary was in a strange town with no friends, and unless they got to the doctor—

They were fools to have gone ahead when they knew they were taking a chance, but nobody expected anything like this. He had worked in mines most of his life and no trouble until now, and then the roof fell in. The whole damned mountain came down—or so it seemed. When he heard the crash, his first thought was for Mary. He was trapped here, but she was trapped out there, and she was alone.

"Better take a rest," Frank said. "We've got some time."

Joe sat down, and Bert looked across at him. "We could work in the dark," he suggested. "That flame eats up air."

Frank shook his head. "If you can't see, there's too much waste effort. You've got to see where the pick goes. Try it with the light a little longer."

Joe's eyes went to Frank. The big man lay tense and still, gripping the rock under his hand. He was in agony, Joe knew it and hated it. Frank was his friend.

"Will we make it, Frank?" He was thinking of Mary. What would she do? What could she do? How could she handle it alone? It wasn't as if they were married. "Think we'll make it?"

"We'll make it," Frank said. "We'll make it, all right."

"Listen!" Bert sat up eagerly. "I think I hear them! Wasn't that the sound of a pick?"

They listened, every muscle tense. There was no sound. Then, far away, some muck shifted. Frank doused the light, and darkness closed in, silent and heavy like the dead, dead air. There was no vibrancy here, no sense of living.

They heard Joe get up, heard the heavy blows of the pick. He worked on and on, his muscles aching with weariness. Each blow and each recovery was an effort. Then Bert spoke, and they heard them change places. Standing once more, Bert could feel the difference. It was much harder to breathe; his lungs labored, and his heart struggled against the walls of his chest, as if to break through. Once he stopped and held a hand over it, frightened.

Long since they had thrown the first two picks aside, their points worn away. They might have to return to them, but now they were using another, sharper pick. They were standing in a hole now. Once a flake of rock fell, and Bert held himself, expecting a crash. It did not come.

Rody moved suddenly. Frank lit the light with a brush of his palm. Rody looked at him, then reached for the pick. "Let me have it," Rody said. "Hell, it's better than sittin' there suckin' my thumb. Give me the pick."

Bert passed it to him; then he staggered to the muck pile and fell, full length, gasping with great throat-rasping gasps.

Rody swung the pick, attacking the bottom of the hole savagely. Sweat ran into his eyes, and he swung, attacking the rock as if it were a flesh-and-blood ene-my, feeling an exultant fury in his blows.

Once he stopped to take five, and looking over at Frank, he said, "How goes it, big boy?"

"Tolerable," Frank said. "You're a good man, Rody."

Rody swelled his chest, and the pick swung easily in his big hands. All of them were lying down now be-cause the air was better close to the muck.

"Hear anything?" Bert asked. "How long will it take them to reach us, Frank?"

"Depends on how much it caved." They had been over this before, but it was hope they needed, any thread of it. Even talking of rescue seemed to bring it nearer. The numbness was all gone now, and his big body throbbed with pain. He fought it, refusing to surrender to it, trying to deny it. He held the pain as though it were some great beast he must overcome.

Suddenly Joe sat up. "Say! What became of the air line for the machine?"

They stared at each other, shocked at their forgetting. "Maybe it ain't busted," Bert said.

Stumbling in his eagerness, Joe fell across the muck, bumping Frank as he did so, jerking an involuntary grunt from him. Then Joe fell on his knees and began clawing rocks away from where the end of the pipe should be, the pipe that supplied compressed air for drilling. He found the pipe and cleared the vent, unscrewing the broken hose to the machine. Trembling, he turned the valve. Cool air shot into the room, and as they breathed deeply, it slowly died away to nothing.

"It will help," Joe said. "Even if it was a little, it will help."

"Damned little," Rody said, "but you're right, Joe. It'll help."

"How deep are you?" Frank asked. He started to shift his body and caught himself with a sharp gasp.

"Four feet—maybe five. She's tough going."

Joe lay with his face close to the ground. The air was close and hot, every breath a struggle. When he breathed, he seemed to get nothing. It left him gasping, struggling for air. The others were the same. Light and air were only a memory now, a memory of some lost paradise.

How long had they been here? Only Frank had a watch, but it was broken, so there was no way of calculating the time. It seemed hours since that crash. Somehow it had been so different from what he had expected. He had believed it would come with a thundering roar, but there was just a splintering sound, a slide of muck, a puff of wind that put their lights out, then a long slide, a trickling of sand, a falling stone. They had lacked even the consolation of drama.

Whatever was to come of it would not be far off now. Whatever happened must be soon. There came no sound, no breath of moving air, only the thick, sticky air and the heat. They were all panting now, gasping for each breath.

Rody sat down suddenly, the pick slipping from his fingers.

"Let me," Joe said.

He swung the pick, then swung it again.

When he stopped, Bert said, "Did you hear something?"

They listened, but there was no sound.

"Maybe they ain't tryin'," Rody said. "Maybe they think we're dead.

"Can you imagine Tom Chambers spendin' his good money to get us out of here?" Rody said. "He don't care. He can get a lot of miners."

Joe thought of those huge, weighted timbers in the Big Stope. Nothing could have held that mass when it started to move. Probably the roof of the Big Stope had collapsed. Up on top there would be a small crowd of waiting people now. Men, women, and children. Still, there wouldn't be so many as in Nevada that time. After all, Bert was the only one down here with children.

But suppose others had been trapped? Why were they thinking they were the only ones?

The dull thud of the pick sounded again. That was Rody back at work. He could tell by the power. He listened, his mind lulled into a sort of hypnotic twilight where there was only darkness and the sound of the pick. He heard the blows, but he knew he was dying. It was no use. He couldn't fight it any longer.

Suddenly the dull blows ceased. Rody said, "Hey! Listen!" He struck again, and it was a dull sound, a hollow sound.

"Hell!" Rody said. "That ain't no ten feet!"

"Let's have some light over here," Rody said, "Frank—?"

He took the light from Frank's hand. The light was down to a feeble flicker now, no longer the proud blade of light that had initially stabbed at the darkness. Rody peered, then passed the lamp back to Frank.

"There should be a staging down there," Frank's voice was clear. "They were running a stopper off it to put in the overhead rounds."

Rody swung, then swung again, and the pick went through. It caught him off balance, and he fell forward, then caught himself. Cool air was rushing into the drift end, and he took the pick and enlarged the hole.

Joe sat up. "God!" he said. "Thank God!"

"Take it easy, you guys, when you go down," Frank said. "That ladder may have been shaken loose by blasting or the cave-in. The top of the ladder is on the left-hand side of the raise. You'll have to drop down to the staging, though, and take the ladder from there. It'll be about an eight- or nine-foot drop."

He tossed a small stone into the hole, and they heard it strike against the boards down below. The flame of the light was bright now as more air came up through the opening. Frank stared at them, sucking air into his lungs.

"Come on, Rody," Joe said. "Lend a hand. We've got to get Frank to a doctor."

"No." Frank's voice was impersonal. "You can't get me down to that platform and then down the ladder. I'd bleed to death before you got me down the raise. You guys go ahead. When they get the drift opened up will be time enough for me. Or maybe when they can come back with a stretcher. I'll just sit here."

"But—" Joe protested.

"Beat it," Frank said.

Bert lowered himself through the opening and dropped. "Come on!" he called. "It's okay!"

Rody followed. Joe hesitated, mopping his face, then looked at Frank, but the big man was staring sullenly at the dark wall.

"Frank—" Joe stopped. "Well, gee—"

He hesitated, then dropped through the hole. From the platform he said, "Frank? I wish—"

His boots made small sounds descending the ladder.

The carbide light burned lower, and the flame flickered as the fuel ran low. Big Frank's face twisted as he tried to move; then his mouth opened very wide, and he sobbed just once. It was all right now. There was no one to hear. Then he leaned back, staring toward the pile of muck, his big hands relaxed and empty.

"Nobody," he muttered. "There isn't anybody, and there never was."

OLD DOC YAK

When I reached San Pedro, I was seventeen, passing as twenty-four, and I'd been on my own for two and a half years. I'd skinned dead cattle in West Texas, worked on a ranch in New Mexico, done assessment work on mining claims in Arizona, worked a few weeks with a circus, and had ridden freight trains from El Paso to the Gulf. From there I'd gone to sea, to the West Indies and Europe. At various places where I'd passed through or worked, I'd fought in the ring eleven times and outside the ring twice as often. Being a stranger in town can be rough.

In San Pedro I had to wait for a ship, so I did whatever came to hand, which wasn't much. Times were hard, and there were ten men for every job, few of which lasted for more than a few hours. The home guards had all the good jobs, and what we outsiders got was just the temporary or fill-in jobs.

Rough painting or bucking rivets in the shipyards, swamping on a truck, or working "standby" on a ship were all a man could find. It was not enough. We all missed meals and slept wherever we could. The town was filled with drifting, homeless men, mostly seamen from all the countries in the world. Sometimes I slept in empty boxcars, in abandoned buildings or in the lumber piles on the old E. K. Wood lumber dock.

There is a neat little bunch of shops on the edge of the ship channel in San Pedro called Port o' Call, but it stands where that lumber dock once stood and where the ships were where the steam schooners used to discharge their deck loads of lumber brought down from Aberdeen, Gray's Harbor, or Coos Bay up on the northwest coast. Sometimes those piles of lumber were so placed that they formed a small cave, a shelter from the rain. I used to wrap newspapers under my coat and sleep there with a soft rain falling and the sounds of traffic on the channel.

Being a seaman with seaman's papers, I sometimes went aboard those steam schooners hunting work and usually managed to stay for a meal. I remember many of them with affection, although some of the names have faded from memory. There were the Yellowstone, the Catherine G. Sudden, and of course, the Humboldt. Long after my own experience with the Humboldt I heard one of those stories that every seaman enjoys.

What the captain's name was, I do not recall, but I knew him slightly. One day I was reciting something by Robert W. Service to a couple of acquaintances, and suddenly a line would not come to me. Then a voice from behind me supplied the line. It was the captain of the Humboldt. I thanked him, and after that we spoke when passing. The story I am about to tell was another thing.

The Humboldt had only the one captain in all her years at sea, and when the ship was retired, the captain retired, also. It was taken to a place (at Terminal Island, I believe) and tied up there to be finally dismantled, but on the night its captain died, the old ship broke its moorings and started out to sea.

Gravely, quietly, and with dignity, the old Humboldt was moving up the channel toward the sea, no steam up and only one light showing.

When the coast guard intercepted her, they found no hand at the wheel and no one on board whom they could see. The old ship was towed back once more and tied up, and true to its nature, it offered no resistance.

How the old ship broke loose, where it was going, and what spirit guided it, no man knew.

Those were hard and lonely days, bitter days, yet each one offered something to what I have done since. There was one man, only a casual contact, whom I disliked intensely, and I have disliked few people. Then I wrote a story about him, and when it was written, I believe I understood him and disliked him no more.

HE WAS A MAN without humor. He seemed somehow aloof, invulnerable. Even his walk was pompous and majestic. He strode with the step of kings and spoke with the voice of an oracle, entirely unaware that his whole being was faintly ludicrous, that those about him were always suspended between laughter and amazed respect.

Someone began calling him Old Doc Yak for no apparent reason, and the name stayed with him. He was a large man, rather portly, wearing a constantly grave expression and given to a pompous manner of speech. His most simple remark was uttered with a sense of earth-shaking import, and a listener invariably held his breath in sheer suspense as he began to speak, only to suffer that sense of frustration one feels when an expected explosion fails to materialize.

His conversation was a garden of the baroque in which biological and geological terms flowered in the most unexpected places. Jim commented once that someone must have thrown a dictionary at him and he got all the words but none of the definitions. We listened in amused astonishment as he would stand, head slightly tilted to one side, an open palm aslant his rather generous stomach, which he would pat affectionately as though in amused approbation of his remarks.

Those were harsh, bitter days. The waterfronts were alive with seamen, all hunting ships. One theme predominated in all our conversations, in all our thoughts, perhaps even in the very pulsing of our blood—how to get by.

No normal brain housed in a warm and sheltered body could possibly conceive of the devious and doubtful schemes contrived to keep soul and body together. Hunger sharpens the wits and renders less effective the moral creeds and codes by which we guide our law-abiding lives. Some of us who were there could even think of the philosophical ramifications of our lives and of our actions. The narrow line that divides the average young man or woman from stealing, begging, or prostitution, is one that has little to do with religion or ethics but only such simple animal necessities as food and shelter. We had been talking of that when Old Doc Yak ventured his one remark.

"I think," he said, pausing portentously, "that any man who will beg, who will so demean himself as to ask for food upon the streets, will stoop to any abomination no matter how low."

He arose, and with a finality that permitted of no reply, turned his back and walked away. It was one of the few coherent statements I ever heard him make, and I watched his broad back, stiff with self-righteousness, as he walked away. I watched, as suddenly speechless as the others.

There was probably not a man present who had not at some time panhandled on the streets. They were a rough, free-handed lot, men who gave willingly when they had it and did not hesitate to ask when in need. All were men who worked, who performed the rough, hard, dangerous work of the world, yet they were men without words, and no reply came to their lips to answer that broad back or the bitter finality of that remark. In their hearts they felt him wrong, for they were sincere men, if not eloquent.

Often after that I saw him on the streets. Always stiff and straight, he never unbent so far as to speak, never appeared even to notice my passing. He paid his way with a careful hand and lived remote from our lonely, uncomfortable world. From meal to meal we had no idea as to the origin of the next, and our nights were spent wherever there was shelter from the wind. Off on the horizon of our hopelessness there was always that miracle—a ship—and endlessly we made the rounds in search of work. Shipping proceeded slowly, and men struggled for the few occasional jobs alongshore. Coming and going on my own quest, I saw men around me drawn fine by hunger, saw their necks become gaunt, their clothing more shabby. It was a bitter struggle to survive in a man-made jungle.

The weeks drew on, and one by one we saw the barriers we had built against hunger slowly fall away. By that time there were few who had not walked the streets looking for the price of a cup of coffee, but even the ready generosity of a seaport town had been strained, and shipping seemed to have fallen off.

One morning a man walked into the Seaman's Institute and fainted away. We had seen him around for days, a quiet young man who seemed to know no one, to have no contacts, too proud to ask for food and too backward to find other means. And then he walked in that morning and crumpled up on the floor like an empty sack.

It was a long moment before any of us moved. We stood staring down at him, and each of us was seeing the specter of his own hunger.

Then Parnatti was arrested. He had been hungry before, and we had heard him say, "I'm going to eat. If I can make it honest, I'll make it, but I'm going to eat regardless." We understood his feelings, although the sentiments were not ours. Contrary to opinion, it is rarely the poor who steal. People do not steal for the necessities but for the embellishments, but when the time came, Parnatti stole a car from a parking lot and sold it. We saw the item in the paper without comfort and then turned almost without hope to the list of incoming ships. Any one of them might need a man; any one of them might save us from tomorrow.

Old Doc Yak seemed unchanged. He came and went as always, as always his phrases bowed beneath a weight of words. I think, vaguely, we all resented him. He was so obviously not a man of the sea, so obviously not one of us. I believe he had been a steward, but stewards were rarely popular in the old days on the merchant ships. Belly robbers, they called them.

Glancing over the paper one afternoon, searching for a ship that might need men, I looked up accidentally just in time to see Old Doc Yak passing a hand over his face. The hand trembled.

For the first time I really saw him. Many times in the past few days we had passed each other on the street, each on his way to survival. Often we had sat in the main room at the Institute, but I had paid little attention. Now, suddenly, I was aware of the change. His vest hung a little slack, and the lines in his face were deeper. For the moment even his pompous manner had vanished. He looked old and tired.

In the ugly jungle of the waterfront the brawl for existence left little time for thinking of anything except the immediate and ever-present need for shelter and food for the body. Old Doc Yak had been nothing more than another bit of waterfront jetsam discarded from the whirl of living into the lazy maelstrom of those alongshore. Now, again, as on that other night, he became an individual, and probably for the first time I saw the man as he was and as he must have seen himself.

Tipped back against the wall, feeling the tightness of my leather jacket across my shoulders, I rubbed the stubble on my unshaved chin and wondered about him. I guess each of us has an illusion about himself. Somewhere inside of himself he has a picture of himself he believes is true. I guess it was that way with Doc. Aloof from those of us who lived around him, he existed in a world of his own creation, a world in which he had importance, a world in which he was somebody. Now, backed into a corner by economic necessity, he was a little puzzled and a little helpless.

Some of us had rented a shack. For six dollars a month we had shelter from the wind and rain, a little chipped crockery, a stove, and a bed. There was a cot in the corner where I slept, and somebody had rustled an old mattress that was stretched out on the deck—floor, I should say. For a dime or perhaps three nickels, if he was good for them, a man could share the bed with three or four others. For a nickel a man got an armful of old newspapers with which he could roll up on the floor. And with the money gathered in such a way we paid another month's rent.

It wasn't much, but it was a corner away from the wind, a place of warmth, and a retreat from the stares of the police and the more favored. Such a place was needed, and never did men return home with more thankfulness than we returned to that shack on its muddy hillside. Men came and went in the remaining weeks of our stay, the strange, drifting motley of the waterfront, men good, bad, and indifferent. Men were there who knew the ports and rivers of a hundred countries, men who knew every sidetrack from Hoboken to Seattle. And then one night Old Doc Yak walked up the path to the door.

There was rain that night, a cold, miserable rain, and a wind that blew it against our thin walls. It was just after ten when the knock came at the door, and when Copper opened it, Old Doc walked in. For a moment his small blue eyes blinked against the light, and then he looked about, a slow distaste growing on his face. There was a sailor's neatness about the place, but it was crude and not at all attractive.

He looked tired, and some of his own neatness was lacking. He might have been fifty-five, but he looked older then, yet his eyes were still remote, unseeing of us, who were the dregs. He looked around again, and we saw his hesitation, sensed the defeat that must have brought him, at last, to this place. But our shack was warm.

"I would like," he said ponderously, "a place to sleep."

"Sure," I said, getting up from the rickety chair I'd tipped against the wall. "There's room in the double bed for one more. It'll cost you a dime."

"You mean," he asked abruptly, and he actually looked at me, "that I must share a bed?"

"Sorry. This isn't the Biltmore. You'll have to share with Copper and Red."

He was on the verge of leaving when a blast of wind and blown rain struck the side of the house, sliding around under the eaves and whining like a wet saw. For an instant he seemed to be weighing the night, the rain and the cold against the warmth of the shack. Then he opened his old-fashioned purse and lifted a dime from its depths.

I say "lifted," and so it seemed. Physical effort was needed to get that dime into my hand, and his fingers released it reluctantly. It was obviously the last of his carefully hoarded supply. Then he walked heavily into the other room and lay down on the bed. It was the first time I had ever seen him lie down, and all his poise seemed suddenly to evaporate, his stiff-necked righteousness seemed to wilt, and all his ponderous posturing with words became empty and pitiful. Lying on the bed with the rain pounding on the roof, he was only an old man, strangely alone.

Sitting in the next room with fire crackling in the stove and the rattling of rain on the windows, I thought about him. Youth and good jobs were behind him, and he was facing a question to which all the ostentatious vacuity of his words gave no reply. The colossal edifice he had built with high-sounding words, the barriers he had attempted to erect between himself and his doubt of himself were crumbling. I put another stick in the stove, watched the fire lick the dampness from its face, and listened to rain beating against the walls and the labored breathing of the man on the bed.

In the washroom of the Seaman's Institute weeks before we had watched him shave. It had been a ritual lacking only incense. The glittering articles from his shaving kit, these had been blocks in the walls of his self-esteem. The careful lathering of his florid cheeks, the application of shaving lotion, these things had been steps in a ritual that never varied. We who were disciples of Gillette and dull blades watched him with something approaching reverence and went away to marvel.

Knowing what must have happened in the intervening weeks, I could see him going to the pawnshop with first one and then another of his prized possessions, removing bit by bit the material things, those glittering silver pieces that shored up his self-vision. Each time his purse would be replenished for a day or two, and as each article passed over the counter into that great maw from which nothing ever returns, I could see some particle of his dignity slipping away. He was a capitalist without capital, a conqueror without conquests, a vocabulary without expression. In the stove the fire crackled; on the wide bed the old man muttered, stirring in his sleep. It was very late.

He did not come again. Several times the following night I walked to the door, almost hoping to see his broad bulk as it labored up the hill. Even Copper looked uneasily out of the window, and Slim took a later walk than usual. We were a group that was closely knit, and though he had not belonged, he had for one brief night been one of us, and when he did not return, we were uneasy.

It was after twelve before Slim turned in. It had been another wet night, and he was tired. He stopped by my chair where I sat reading a magazine.

"Listen," he said, flushing a little, "if he comes, Old Doc, I mean, I'll pay if he ain't got the dime. He ain't such a bad guy."

"Sure," I said. "Okay."

He didn't come. The wind whined and snarled around the corners of the house, and we heard the tires of a car whine on the wet pavement below. It is a terrible thing to see a man's belief in himself crumble, for when one loses faith in one's own illusion, there is nothing left. Even Slim understood that. It was almost daybreak before I fell asleep.

Several nights drifted by. There was food to get, and the rent was coming due. We were counting each dime, for we had not yet made the six dollars. There was still a gap, a breach in our wall that we might not fill. And outside was the night, the rain, and the cold.

The *Richfield,* a Standard tanker, was due in. I had a shipmate aboard her, and when she came up the channel, I was waiting on the dock. They might need an A.B.

They didn't.

It was a couple of hours later when I climbed the hill toward the shack. I didn't often go that way, but this time it was closer, and I was worried. The night before I'd left the money for the rent in a thick white cup on the cupboard shelf. And right then murder could be done for five bucks. Accidentally I glanced in the window. Then I stopped.

Old Doc Yak was standing by the cupboard, holding the white cup in his hand. As I watched, he dipped his fingers in and drew out some of our carefully gleaned nickels, dimes, and quarters. Then he stood there letting those shining metal disks trickle through his thick fingers and back into the cup. Then he dipped his fingers again, and I stood there, holding my breath.

A step or two and I could have stopped him, but I stood there, gripped by his indecision, half guessing what was happening inside him. Here was money.

Here, for a little while, was food, a room, a day or two of comfort. I do not think he considered the painstaking effort to acquire those few coins or the silent, bedraggled men who had trooped up the muddy trail to add a dime or fifteen cents to the total of our next month's rent. What hunger had driven him back, I knew. What helplessness and humiliation waited in the streets below, I also knew.

Slowly, one by one, the coins dribbled back into the cup, the cup was returned to the shelf, and Old Doc Yak turned and walked from the door. For one moment he paused, his face strangely gray and old, staring out across the bleak, rain-washed roofs toward the gray waters of the channel and Terminal Island just beyond.

Then he walked away, and I waited until he was out of sight before I went inside, and I, who had seen so much of weariness and defeat, hesitated before I took down the cup. It was all there, and suddenly I was a little sorry that it was.

Once more I saw him. One dark, misty night I came up from the lumber docks, collar turned up, cap pulled low, picking my way through the shadows and over the railroad ties, stumbling along rails lighted only by the feeble red and green of switch lights. Reaching the street, I scrambled up the low bank and saw him standing in the light of a street lamp.

He was alone, guarded from friendship as always by his icy impenetrability but somehow strangely pathetic with his sagging shoulders and graying hair. I started to speak, but he turned up his coat collar and walked away down a dark street.

SURVIVAL

There are many men like Tex Worden, and they can be found doing their share of the hard work of the world wherever they may be. They make excellent soldiers or sailors and have courage of an uncommon quality but do not think of it as such. Not one of them would apply the term hero to himself or think of himself in connection with the term (or anyone else, when it came to that!), but they do the job they are hired to do as best they know how.

By and large they are very good at what they do, are inclined to be a little impatient with those less capable than themselves, but will take time to instruct anyone who shows an inclination to learn and a readiness to lend a hand. They are never flamboyant, and they do not flock with others of their kind or with anyone else. You would never find one of them making a profession of fighting (except in the services), but if you get into a fight with one, you would have to half kill him to win.

The events of this story are basically true, and I knew the "Tex Worden" written about here. That was not his name, and the circumstances were a little different. I knew him in Pedro and made a trip to sea in the same forecastle.

Track Down And Capture Exciting Western Adventure!

WANTED!

LOUIS L'AMOUR COLLECTION!

REWARD OFFERED

Mail your "WANTED" poster today. (see inside)

Make your "wanted" claim and receive your rightful reward!

• A free authentic Louis L'Amour calendar!

• A free preview of the bestselling SACKETT

And much more…

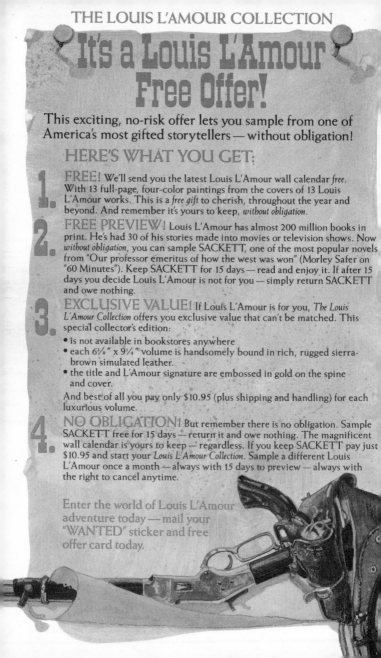

FREE — MAGNIFICENT WALL CALENDAR!
FREE — PREVIEW OF SACKETT

- No Obligation!   • No Purchase Necessary!

Yes! I'm claiming my reward!

"WANTED!" STICKER GOES HERE

Send SACKETT for 15 days free! If I keep this volume, I will pay just $10.95 plus shipping and handling. Future Louis L'Amour Westerns will be sent to me about once a month, on a 15-day, Free-Examination basis. I understand that there is no minimum number of books to buy, and I may cancel my subscription at any time. The Free Louis L'Amour wall calendar is mine to keep even if I decide to return SACKETT.

NAME _____

ADDRESS _____

CITY _____

STATE _____ ZIP _____

MY NO RISK GUARANTEE:

There's no obligation to buy. The free calendar is mine to keep. I may preview SACKETT and any other Louis L'Amour book for 15 days. If I don't want it, I simply return the book and owe nothing. If I keep it, I pay only $10.95 (plus postage and handling).

70136

IL123

Track down and capture exciting western adventure from one of America's foremost novelists!

• It's free! • No obligation! • Exclusive value!

TEX WORDEN shoved his way through the crowd in the Slave Market and pushed his book under the wicket.

The clerk looked up, taking in his blistered face and swollen hands. "What'll you have, buddy? You want to register?"

"Naw, I'm here to play a piano solo, what d'you think?"

"Wise guy, eh?"

Tex's eyes were cold. "Sure, and what about it?"

"You guys all get too smart when you get ashore. I'm used to you guys, but one of these days I'm going to come out from behind here and kick hell out of one of you!"

"Why not now?" Worden said mildly. "You don't see me out there running down the street, do you? You just come out from behind that counter, and I'll lay you in the scuppers."

At a signal from the man behind the wicket a big man pushed his way through the crowd and tapped Tex Worden on the shoulder. "All right, buddy, take it easy. You take it easy, or you get the boot."

"Yeah?"

"Yeah!"

Tex grinned insultingly and turned his back, waiting for the return of his book. The clerk opened it grudgingly, then looked up, startled.

"You were on the *Raratonga!*"

"So what?"

"We heard only one of the crew was saved!"

"Who the hell do you think I am? Napoleon? And

that saved business, that's the bunk. That's pure ma-
larkey. I saved myself. Now come on, get that book
fixed. I want to get out of here."

The plainclothes man was interested. "No kiddin',
are you Tex Worden?"

"I am."

"Hell, man, that must have been some wreck. The
papers say that if it wasn't for you none of them would
have gotten back. Dorgan was on that boat, too!"

"Dorgan?" Tex turned to face him. "You know
Dorgan?"

"*Knew* him? I should say I did! A tough man, too.
One of the toughest."

Worden just looked at him. "How tough a man is
often depends on where he is and what's he's doing."
He was looking past the plainclothes man, searching
for a familiar face. In all this gathering of merchant
seamen hunting work, he saw no one.

Times were hard. There were over seven hundred
seamen on the beach, and San Pedro had become a
hungry town. Jobs were scarce, and a man had to wait
his turn. And he didn't have eating money. Everything
he had had gone down with the *Raratonga*. He had
money coming to him, but how long it would be before
he saw any of it was a question.

Near the door he glimpsed a slight, buck-toothed
seaman in a blue pea jacket whose face looked familiar. He edged through the crowd to him. "Hi, Jack,
how's about staking a guy to some chow?"

"Hey? Don't I know you? Tex, isn't it?"

"That's right. Tex Worden. You were on the *West
Ivis* when I was."

"Come on, there's a greasy spoon right down the
street." When they were outside, he said, "I don't want
to get far from the shipping office. My number's due to
come up soon."

"How long's it been?"

"Three months. Well, almost that. Times are rough,

Tex." He looked at Worden. "What happened to you?"

"I was on the *Raratonga*."

The sailor shook his head in awe. "*Jee-sus!* You were the only one who came back!"

"Some passengers made it. Not many but some."

"How's it feel to be a hero? And with Hazel Ryan yet. And Price! The actress and the millionaire! You brought them back alive."

"Me an' Frank Buck. If this is how it feels to be a hero, you can have it. I'm broke. There's a hearing today, and maybe I can hit up the commissioner for a few bucks."

The other seaman thrust out a hand. "I'm Conrad, Shorty Conrad. Paid off a ship from the east coast of South America, and I lied to you. It didn't take me three months because I've got a pal back there. I'll say a word for you, and maybe you can get a quick ship-out."

They ordered coffee and hamburger steaks. "This is a tough town, man. No way to get out of this dump unless you can take a pierhead jump or get lucky. If you know a ship's officer who'll ask for you, you got a better chance."

"I don't know nobody out here. I been shipping off the east coast."

A burly Greek came along behind the counter. He stared hard at them. "You boys got money? I hate to ask, but we get stiffed a lot."

"I got it." Shorty showed him a handful of silver dollars. "Anyway, this is Tex Worden. He was on the *Raratonga*."

"You got to be kiddin'."

The Greek eyed him with respect. "That where you got blistered?" he motioned toward Worden's hands. "What happened to them?"

"Knittin'," Tex said. "Them needles get awful heavy after a while."

He was tired, very, very tired. The reaction was beginning to set in now. He was so tired he felt he'd fall off the stool if he wasn't careful, and he didn't even have the price of a bed. If he hit the sack now, he'd probably pass out for a week. His shoulders ached, and his hands were sore. They hurt when he used them, and they hurt just as much when he didn't.

"It was a nasty blow, Shorty. You never saw wind like that."

"She went down quick, eh? I heard it was like fifteen minutes."

"Maybe. It was real quick. Starb'rd half door give way, and the water poured in; then a bulkhead give way, and the rush of water put the fires out. No power, no pumps—it was a madhouse."

They were silent, sipping their coffee and eating the greasy steaks. Finally Shorty asked, "How long were you out there?"

"Fifteen days, just a few miles off the equator. It rained once—just in time."

Faces of men he knew drifted by the door. He knew some of them but could not recall their names. They were faces he'd seen from Hong Kong to Hoboken, from Limehouse to Malay Street in Singapore or Grant Road in Bombay, Gomar Street in Suez, or the old American Bar on Lime Street in Liverpool. He'd started life as a cowboy but now he'd been at sea for fifteen years.

It was a rough crowd out there on Beacon Street, but if he did not know them all, he knew their kind. There were pimps and prostitutes, seamen, fishermen, longshoremen, and bums, but they were all people, and they were all alive, and they were all walking on solid ground.

There were gobs there from the battle wagons off Long Beach and girls who followed the fleet. There was an occasional drunk looking for a live wire who might spring for another bottle, and he liked it.

"Maybe I'll save my money," he said aloud, "buy myself a chicken ranch. I'd like to own a chicken ranch near Modesto."

"Where's Modesto?"

"I don't know. Somewhere north of here. I just like the sound of it."

Tex Worden looked down at his hands. Under the bandages they were swollen with angry red cracks where the blisters had been and some almost raw flesh that had just begun to heal. In the mirror he saw a face like a horror mask, for tough as his hide was, the sun had baked it to an angry red that he could not touch to shave. He looked frightening and felt worse. If only he could get some sleep!

He did not want to think of those bitter, brutal days when he rowed the boat, hour after hour, day after day, rowing with a sullen resignation, all sense of time forgotten, even all sense of motion. There had been no wind for days, just a dead calm, the only movement being the ripples in the wake of the lifeboat.

He got up suddenly. "I almost forgot. I got to stop by the commissioner's office. They want to ask me some questions. Sort of a preliminary inquiry, I guess."

Shorty stole a quick look at him. "Tex—you be careful. Be real careful. These aren't seamen. They don't know what it's like out there. They can't even imagine."

"I'll be all right."

"Be careful, I tell you. I read something about it in the papers. If you ain't careful they'll crucify you."

There were several men in business suits in the office when they entered. They all looked at Tex, but the commissioner was the only one who spoke. "Thank you, son. That was a good job you did out there."

"It was my job," Tex said. "I done what I was paid for."

The commissioner dropped into a swivel chair behind his desk. "Now, Worden, I expect you're tired. We will not keep you any longer than we must, but naturally we must arrive at some conclusions as to what took place out there and what caused the disaster. If there is anything you can tell us, we'd be glad to hear it."

Shorty stole a glance at the big man with the red face. A company man, here to protect their interests. He knew the type.

"There's not much to tell, sir. I had come off watch about a half hour before it all happened, and when I went below, everything seemed neat and shipshape. When the ship struck, I was sitting on my bunk in the fo'c's'le taking off my shoes.

"The jolt threw me off the bench, an' Stu fell off his bunk on top of me. He jumped up an' said, 'What the hell happened?' and I said I didn't know, but it felt like we hit something. He said, 'It's clear enough outside, and we're way out to sea. Must be a derelict!' I was pulling on my shoes, and so was he, an' we ran up on deck.

"There was a lot of running around, and we started forward, looking for the mate. Before we'd made no more than a half-dozen steps, the signal came for boat stations, and I went up on the boat deck. Last I saw of Stu he was trying to break open a jammed door, and I could hear people behind it.

"We must have hit pretty hard because she was starting to settle fast, going down by the head with a heavy list to starb'rd. I was mighty scared because I remembered that starb'rd half door, and—"

"What about the half door, Worden? What was wrong with it?"

"Nothing at all, commissioner," the company man interrupted. "The company inspector—"

"Just a minute, Mr. Winstead." The commissioner spoke sharply. "Who is conducting this inquiry?"

"Well, I—"

"Proceed with your story, Worden."

"The half door was badly sprung, sir. Somebody said the ship had been bumped a while back, and I guess they paid no mind to repairs. Anyway, it wasn't no bother unless they was loaded too heavy, and—"

"What do you mean, Worden? Was the ship overloaded?"

Winstead scowled at Worden, his lips drawing to a thin, angry line.

"Well, sir, I guess I ain't got no call to speak, but—"

"You just tell what happened at the time of the wreck, Worden. That will be sufficient!" Winstead said, interrupting.

"Mr. Winstead! I will thank you not to interrupt this man's story again. I am conducting this inquiry, and regardless of the worth of what Worden may have to say, he is the sole remaining member of the crew. As a seafaring man of many years' experience, he understands ships, and he was there when it happened. I intend to hear *all*—let me repeat, *all*—he has to say. We certainly are not going to arrive at any conclusions by concealing anything. If your vessel was in proper condition, you have nothing to worry about, but I must say your attitude gives rise to suspicion." He paused, glancing up at the reporters who were writing hurriedly. "Now, Worden, if you please. Continue your story."

"Well, sir, I was standing by number three hatch waiting for the last loads to swing aboard so's I could batten down the hatch, an' I heard Mr. Jorgenson—he was the mate—say to Mr. Winstead here that he didn't like it at all. He said loading so heavy with that bad door was asking for trouble, and he went on to mention that bad bulkhead amidships.

"I don't know much about it, sir, except what he said and the talk in the fo'c's'le about the bulkhead between hatches three and four. One of the men who'd been chipping rust down there said you didn't dare chip very hard or you'd drive your hammer right through, it was that thin. When I was ashore clearing the gangway, I saw she was loaded down below the Plimsoll marks."

"Weren't you worried, Worden? I should think that knowing the conditions you would have been."

"No, sir. Generally speaking, men working aboard ship don't worry too much. I've been going to sea quite a while now, and it's always the other ships that sink, never the one a fellow's on. At least that's the way it is until something happens. We don't think about it much, and if she sinks, then she sinks, and that's all there is to it."

"I see."

"Yes, sir. There was trouble with that half door before we were three days out. Me an' a couple of others were called to help Chips caulk that half door. You know—it's a door in the ship's side through which cargo is loaded. Not all ships have 'em. That door had been rammed some time or another, and it didn't fit right. In good weather or when she carried a normal load it was all right.

"But three days out we had a spot of bad weather; some of that cargo shifted a mite, and she began to make water, so we had to recaulk that door.

"To get back to that night, sir. When I got to my boat station, I saw one of the officers down on the deck with his head all stove in. I don't know whether he got hit with something or whether it was done by the bunch of passengers who were fighting over the boat. Ever'body was yellin' an' clawin', so I waded in an' socked a few of them and got them straightened out.

"I told them they'd damn well better do what they were told because I was the only one who knew how to get that lifeboat into the water. After that they quieted down some. A couple of them ran off aft, hunting another boat, but I got busy with the lifeboat cover.

"All of a sudden it was still, so quiet it scared you. The wind still blowing and big waves all around but ghostly still. You could hear a body speak just like I'm speakin' now. It was like everything quieted down to let us die in peace. I could tell by the feel of her that we hadn't long. She was settlin' down, and she had an ugly, heavy feel to her.

"Mister, that was a tryin' time. All those people who'd been yellin' an' fightin' stood there lookin' at me, and one little fellow in a gray suit—he had a tie on, an' everything. He was Jewish, I think. He asked me what he could do, and I told him to get to the other end of the boat, to loose the falls and lower away when I did.

"I got the boat cover off, and we got the boat into the water, and the ship was down so far and canted over—a bad list to her—that it was no problem gettin' those few folks into the lifeboat.

"I took a quick look around. The boat longside was already in the water, and there were two A.B.s with it, Fulton an' Jaworski, it was. They had maybe thirty people in that boat, and I saw one of the stewards there, too. There was nobody else in sight, but I could hear some yelling forward.

"Just then she gave a sort of shudder, and I jumped into the boat and told the Jew to cast off. He had trouble because she was rising and falling on the water, but a woman helped him. I didn't know who she was then, but later I found out it was that actress, Hazel Ryan.

"We shoved off, and I got oars into the water, and we started looking for others. When we got out a ways, I could see Sparks—one of them, anyway, in the radio shack.

"Then the ship gave a kind of lunge and went down by the head. She just dipped down and then slid right away, going into the water on her beam ends with all the port-side boats just danglin' there, useless, as they couldn't be got into the water. At the last minute, as she went under, I saw a man with an ax running from boat to boat cutting the falls. He was hoping they'd come up floating, and two or three of them did.

"All of a sudden I see a man in the water. He was a pleasant-looking man with gray hair, and he was swimming. He looked so calm I almost laughed. 'Cold, isn't it?' he says, and then he just turns and swims away, cool as you please. You'd have thought the beach wasn't fifty feet away.

"It's things like that fairly take your wind, sir, and there I was, trying to pull the lifeboat away from the ship and hopin' for the best.

"I turned my head once and looked back. Mostly I was trying to guide the boat through wreckage that was already afloat. When I looked back—this was just before she went under—I glimpsed somebody standin' on the bridge, one arm through the pilot-house window to hang on, and he was lighting his pipe with his free hand.

"It just didn't seem like it could be happening. There I was just minutes before, a-comin' off watch, all set for a little shuteye, and now here I was in a lifeboat, and the ship was goin' down.

"There must have been nearly a hundred people in the water and not a whisper out of any of them. Like they was all in shock or somethin' of the kind. Once a guy did yell to somebody else. Then something exploded under water—maybe the boilers busted. I wouldn't know. Anyway, when it was over, a lot of those folks who'd been in the water were gone. I fetched the bow of my boat around and rowed toward something white floating in the water. It was a woman, and I got her into the boat."

"Was that Hazel Ryan?" a reporter asked.

"No, it was Lila, a stewardess. Then I held the boat steady whilst another man climbed in. He pointed out three people clingin' to a barrel. I started for them.

"The sea was rough, and folks would disappear behind a wave, and sometimes when you looked, they weren't there anymore. Those people were havin' a time of it, tryin' to hang to that barrel, so I got to them first, and folks helped them aboard. The Ryan woman was one of them.

"I'll give her this. First moment she could speak, she asked if there was anything she could do, and I said just to set quiet and try to get warm. If I needed help, I'd ask for it.

"It was funny how black everything was, yet you could see pretty well for all of that. You'd see a white face against the black water, and by the time you got there, it was gone.

"One time I just saw an arm. Woman's, I think it was. She was right alongside the boat, and I let go an oar an' grabbed for her, but her arm slipped right through my fingers, and she was gone.

"Some of those we'd picked up were in panic and some in shock. That little Jewish fellow with the neck-tie and all, he didn't know a thing about the sea, but he was cool enough. We moved people around, got the boat trimmed, and I got her bow turned to meet the sea and started to try to ride her out."

"What about the radio?"

"We didn't think about that for long. At least I didn't. There hadn't been much time, and the chances were slim that any message got off. It all happened too fast.

"Sparks was in there, and he was sending. I am sure of that, but he hadn't any orders, and most shipmasters don't want any May Day or SOS goin' out unless they say. If he sent it, he sent it on his own because the old man never made the bridge."

"The man you saw lighting his pipe?"

"Jorgenson, I think. He was watch officer, but they were changing watch, so I don't know. He wasn't heavy enough for the old man.

"Anyway, I'd no time to think of them. The sea was making up, and I was havin' the devil's own time with that boat. She'd have handled a lot easier if we'd had a few more people aboard.

"Lila, she was hurting. Seemed like she was all stove up inside, and the shock was wearing off. She was feeling pain, turning and twisting like, and the Ryan woman was trying to help. She and that little Jew, they worked over her, covering her with coats, trying to tuck them under so she'd ride easier. The rest just sat and stared."

"No other boats got off?"

"I don't know—except that boat with Fulton and Jaworski. They were good men, and they'd do what could be done. The ship had taken a bad list, so I don't think many of the boats on the topside could be launched at all."

"How was the weather?"

"Gettin' worse, sir. There was nobody to spell me on the oars because nobody knew anything about handling a boat in a heavy sea. I shipped the oars and got hold of the tiller, which made it a mite easier.

"Lila had passed out; spray was whipping over the boat. I was hanging to that tiller, scared ever' time a big one came over that it would be the last of us. There was no way to play. You just had to live from one sea to the next."

"How long did the storm last?"

"About two days. I don't rightly remember because I was so tired everything was hazy. When the sea calmed down enough, I let Schwartz have the tiller. I'd been gripping it so hard and so long I could hardly let go."

"You were at the tiller forty-eight hours without relief?"

"Yes, sir. Maybe a bit more. But after that she began to settle down, and the sun came out."

"The boat was provisioned according to regulations?"

"Yes, sir. We'd some trouble about water later but not much."

"How about the crew and the officers? Were they efficient in your opinion?"

"Sure. Yes, they were okay. I've been going to sea quite a spell, and I never have seen any seaman or officer shirk his job. It ain't bravery nor lack of it, just that he knows his job and has been trained for it.

"Sometimes you hear about the crew rushing the boats or being inefficient. I don't believe it ever happens. They're trained for the job, and it is familiar to them. They know what they are to do, and they do it.

"Passengers are different. All of a sudden everything is different. There's turmoil an' confusion; there's folks runnin' back and forth, and the passengers don't know what's going on.

"Sometimes one of them will grab a crewman and yell something at him, and the crewman will pull loose and go about his business. The passenger gets mad and thinks they've been deserted by the crew when chances are that seaman had something to do. Maybe his boat station was elsewhere. Maybe he'd been sent with a message for the engineer on watch below.

"Maybe when those crewmen you hear about rushing the boats are just getting there to get the boat cover off and clear the falls. This wasn't my first wreck, and I've yet to see a crewman who didn't stand by."

"How long before she sank?"

"Fifteen minutes, give or take a few. It surely wasn't more, though. It might have been no more than five. We'd made quite a bit of water before the cargo shifted and she heeled over. With that half door under water—well, I figure that door gave way and she just filled up and sank."

"Mr. Commissioner?" Winstead asked. "I'd like permission to ask this man a few questions. There are a few matters I'd like to clear up."

"Go ahead."

"Now, my man, if you'd be so kind. How many were in the boat when you got away from the scene of the wreck?"

"Eight."

"Yet when you were picked up by the *Maloaha* there were but three?"

"Yes."

"How do you account for that?"

"Lila—she was the stewardess—she died. Like I said, she'd been hurt inside. She was a mighty good woman, and I hated to see her go. Clarkson—he went kind of screwy. Maybe he didn't have all his buttons to start with. Anyway, he got kind of wild and kept staring at a big shark who was following us. One night he grabbed up a boat hook and tried to get that shark. It was silly. That shark was just swimmin' along in hopes. No use to bother him. Well, he took a stab at that shark and fell over the side.

"Handel, he just sat an' stared. Never made no word for anybody, just stared. He must've sat that way for eight or nine days. We all sort of lost track of time, but he wouldn't take water, wouldn't eat a biscuit. He just sat there, hands hanging down between his knees.

"I'd rigged a sort of mast from a drifting stick and part of a boat cover. The mast this boat should have carried was missing. Anyway, the little sail I rigged gave us some rest, and it helped. Late one day we were moving along at a pretty fair rate for us when I saw a squall coming. She swept down on us so quick that I gave the tiller to Schwartz and stumbled forward to get that sail down before we swamped. With the wind a-screaming and big seas rolling up, I'd almost reached the sail when this Handel went completely off his course. He jumped up and grabbed me, laughing and singing, trying to dance with me or something.

"Struggling to get free, I fell full length in the boat, scrambled up and pulled that sail down, and when I looked around, Handel was gone."

"Gone?" Winstead said.

"You mean—over the side?" the commissioner asked.

"That's right. Nearest thing I could figure out was that when I fell, he fell, too. Only when I fell into the bottom, he toppled over the side.

"Rain and blown spray was whipping the sea, and we couldn't see him. No chance to turn her about. We'd have gone under had we tried.

"For the next ten hours we went through hell, just one squall after another, and all of us had to bail like crazy just to keep us afloat."

"So," Winstead said, "you killed a passenger?"

"I never said that. I don't know what happened. Whatever it was, it was pure accident. I'd nothing against the man. He was daffy, but until that moment he'd been harmless. I figure he didn't mean no harm then, only I had to get free of him to save the boat."

"At least, that is your story?"

"Mister, with a ragin' squall down on us there was no time to coddle nobody. I didn't have a strait jacket nor any way to get him into one. It was save the boat or we'd all drown."

"Yet even with your small sail up, you might have lasted, might you not?"

Worden considered the matter, then he shrugged. "No way to tell. I was the only seaman aboard, and it was my judgment the sail come down. I'd taken it down."

"All right. We will let that rest for the moment. That accounts for three. Now what became of the other two?"

"The Jew—Schwartz, he come to me in the night a few days later. We were lyin' in a dead calm, and most of our water was gone. Sky was clear, not a cloud in sight, and we'd a blazin' hot day ahead. He told me he was goin' over the side, and he wanted me to know because he didn't want me to think he was a quitter.

"Hell, that little kike had more guts than the whole outfit. I told him nothing doing. Told him I needed him, which was no lie. It was a comfort just to have him there because what he didn't know he could understand when I told him. He wouldn't accept the fact that I needed him.

"It even came to the point where I suggested I toss a coin with him to see who went over. He wouldn't listen to that, and we both knew I was talkin' nonsense. I was the only seaman. The only one who could handle a boat. It was my job to bring that boat back with as many people as possible. I ain't goin' for any of that hero stuff. That's all baloney. Sure, I wanted to live as much as any man, but I had a job to do. It was what I signed on to do. At least when I signed on, it was to do a seaman's job. I ain't done nothing I wouldn't do again."

"I see. And what became of the other man?"

"He was a big guy, and he was tough. He tried to take charge of the boat. There's a lot happens in an open boat like that when everybody is close to shovin' off for the last time. People just ain't thinkin' the way they should. This big guy, he had more stamina than the rest of them. Most of them tried to take a hand in rowin' the boat.

"We'd no wind, you see, and I was hopin' we could get out of the calm into the wind again, but he wouldn't do anything. He just sat. He said I was crazy, that I was goin' the wrong way. He said I drank water at night when they were all asleep. Twice when I passed water forward for somebody else, he drank it.

"Then one night I woke up with him pourin' the last

of our water down his damn throat. The Ryan woman, she was tuggin' at his arm to try to stop him, but hell, it was too late.

"It was her callin' to me that woke me up, and I went at him. He emptied the cask and threw it over the side. I tried to stop him, and we had it out, right there. He was some bigger than me and strong, but there was no guts to him. I smashed him up some and put him between the oars. I told him to row, that he'd live as long as he rowed. First we had to circle around and pick up the cask."

"An empty cask?" Winstead asked incredulously. "What in God's world did you do that for?"

"Mister, it's only in the movies where some guy on the desert an' dyin' of thirst throws away a canteen because it's empty. Shows how little some of those screenwriters know. Supposin' he finds water next day? How's he goin' to carry it?

"You throw away an empty canteen in the desert an' you're committin' suicide. Same thing out there. We might get a rain squall, and if we did, we'd need something to hold water. So we circled and picked up that cask."

"And what happened to Dorgan?"

Tex Worden's face was bleak. "He quit rowin' twenty-four hours before we got picked up."

Winstead turned to the commissioner. "Sir, this man has admitted to killing one passenger; perhaps he killed two or three. As to his motives—I think they will appear somewhat different under cross-examination.

"I have evidence as to this man's character. He is known along the waterfronts as a tough. He frequents houses of ill fame. He gets into drunken brawls. He has been arrested several times for fighting. His statements here today have cast blame upon the company. I intend to produce evidence that this man is not only a scoundrel but an admitted murderer!"

Tex sat up slowly.

"Yes, I've been arrested for fighting. Sometimes when I come ashore after a long cruise I have a few too many, and sometimes I fight, but it's always with my own kind. After a trip on one of those louse-bound scows of yours, a man has to get drunk. But I'm a seaman. I do my job. There's never a man I've worked with will deny that. I'm sorry you weren't in that boat with us so you could have seen how it was.

"You learn a lot about people in a lifeboat. Me, I never claimed to be any psalm singer. Maybe the way I live isn't your way, but when the times comes for the men to step out, I'll be there. I'll be doin' my job.

"It's easy to sit around on your fat behinds and say what you'd have done or what should have been done. You weren't there.

"Nobody knows what he'd do until he's in the spot. I was the only guy in that boat knew a tiller from a thwart. It was me bring that boat through or nobody. I'd rather lose two than lose them all. I wasn't doin' it because it was swell of me or because they'd call me a hero. I was bringin' them in because it was my job.

"Handel now. He wasn't responsible. Somethin' happened to him that he never expected. He could have lived his life through a nice, respected man, but all of a sudden it isn't the same anymore. There's nobody to tell to do something or to even ask. He's caught in a place he can't see his way out of. He'd never had just to *endure,* and there was nothing in him to rise to the surface and make him stand up. It sort of affected his mind.

"Hazel Ryan? She has moxie. When I told her it was her turn to row, she never hesitated, and I had to make her quit. She wasn't all that strong, but she was game. A boatload like her an' I could have slept half-way back.

"Dorgan was a bad apple. The whole boat was on edge because of him. He'd been used to authority and was a born bully. He was used to takin' what he wanted an' lettin' others cry about it. I told him what he had to do, and he did it after we had our little set-to."

"Who did you think you were, Worden? God? With the power of life and death?"

"Listen, mister"—Worden leaned forward—"when I'm the only seaman in the boat, when we have damn' little water, an' we're miles off the steamer lanes, when there's heat, stillness, thirst, an' we're sittin' in the middle of a livin' hell, you can just bet I'm Mister God as far as that boat's concerned.

"The company wasn't there to help. You weren't there to help, nor was the commissioner. Sure, the little fat guy prayed, an' Clarkson prayed. Me, I rowed the boat."

He lifted his hands, still swollen and terribly lacerated where the blisters had broken to cracks in the raw flesh. "Forty hours," he said, "there at the end I rowed for forty hours, tryin' to get back where we might be picked up. We made it.

"We made it," he repeated, "but there was a lot who didn't."

The commissioner rose, and Winstead gathered his papers, his features set and hard. He threw one quick, measuring glance at Worden.

"That will be all, gentlemen," the commissioner said. "Worden, you will remain in port until this is straightened out. You are still at the same address?"

"Yes, sir. At the Seaman's Institute."

Shorty glanced nervously out the window, then at Winstead. Tex turned away from the desk, a tall, loose figure in a suit that no longer fit. Winstead left, saying nothing, but as Worden joined Shorty, the commissioner joined them.

"Worden?"

"Yes, sir?"

"As man to man, and I was once a seaman myself,

Mr. Winstead has a lot of influence. He will have the best attorney money can hire, and to a jury off the shore things do not look the same as in a drifting lifeboat.

"The *Lichenfield* docked a few minutes ago, and she will sail after refueling. I happen to know they want two A.B.s This is unofficial, of course. The master of the vessel happens to be a friend of mine."

They shook hands briefly.

There was a faint mist falling when they got outside. Tex turned up his coat collar. Shorty glanced toward Terminal Island. "You got an outfit? Some dungarees an' stuff?"

"I'd left a sea bag at the Institute." He touched the blue shirt. "This was in it. I can draw some gear from the slop chest."

"They got your tail in a crack, Tex. What's next, the *Lichenfield?*"

"Well," he said shortly, "I don't make my living in no courtroom."

THICKER THAN
BLOOD

One shipped out of San Pedro in those days through what was called the Marine Service Bureau. Less politely, the seamen referred to it as Fink Hall or the Slave Market. Upon arrival in port it was customary to register there and wait one's turn. At the time that was about three months. However, when I did leave San Pedro, it was by taking what the old wind-ship sailors used to call a 'pierhead jump.' I shipped off the dock.

The Seaman's Institute maintained a dormitory for seamen ashore, a reading room, a game room, and a mailing address. Some of the best checker playing I ever saw was done there. On Wednesday nights there was entertainment.

When I arrived at the Institute on that last night, none of the regulars was around. It was damp and cold outside, and I had but five cents in my pocket. Turning a newspaper to the shipping lists, I started checking to see what ships were arriving and where they were bound.

A stranger loomed over me, asking, "What's the best way to get to Wilmington at this hour?"

"Walk," I said, "unless you've money enough for a cab." I explained the best route. "But watch yourself. If you've got two dimes, don't let them rattle or you'll get rolled for them."

"I've got a ship. They're coming in to take on fuel oil, and they radioed ahead for an able seaman."

"You're lucky."

"Why not come along? They might need another man."

It was worth the gamble, and I'd no place to go and no place to sleep.

It was a dark night with a light drizzle veiling the lights on the Luckenbach dock across the channel. I took turns carrying his sea bag, as I'd none of my own. If I did ship out, I'd have to buy my outfit from the ship's slop chest.

The ship was a freighter outward bound for the Far East, and it was due in at midnight. We were a few minutes late, but it had not arrived. We sat down under the eaves of the warehouse to wait, and it was after four in the morning before we finally saw it, creeping up the channel.

We went aboard and were signed on in the chief mate's cabin with the only light the reading lamp over his desk. I had no idea what I was getting into, but it made no difference. I was broke, and this was a job.

That ship was to be my home for the next six months, and before I arrived back in the States, I'd have been to Yokohama, Kobe, Nagasaki, Shanghai, Hong Kong, and various ports in Borneo, Java, Sumatra, and the Malay States as well as Singapore. With stops here and there we went on around the world to finally pay off in Brooklyn.

HE HAD IT COMING if ever a man did, and I could have killed him then and nobody the wiser. If he had been man enough, we could have gone off on the dock and slugged it out, and everything would have been settled either way the cat jumped. There's nothing like a sock on the chin to sort of clean things up. It saves hard feelings and time wasted in argument. But Duggs was the chief mate, who wasn't man enough to whip me and knew it.

Bilge water, they say, is thicker than blood, and once men have been shipmates, no matter how much they hate each other's guts, they stand together against the world. That's the way it is supposed to be, but it certainly wasn't going to be that way with Duggs and me. I decided that in a hurry.

From the hour I shipped on that freighter, Duggs made it tough for me, but it wasn't only me but the whole crew. You don't mind so much if a really tough guy makes you like it, but when a two-by-twice scenery bum like Duggs rubs it into you just because he has the authority, it just naturally hurts.

If we'd gone off on the dock where it was man to man, I'd have lowered the boom on his chin and left him for the gulls to pick over. But we were aboard ship, and if you sock an officer aboard ship, it's your neck.

Sometimes I think he laid awake nights figuring ways to be nasty, but maybe he didn't have to go to that much effort. I suspect it just came naturally. He made it rough for all of us but particularly me. Not that I didn't have my chances to cool him off. I had three of them. The first was at sea, the second in Port Swettenham, and the third—well, you'll hear about that.

Every dirty job he could find fell to Tony or me, and he could think of more ways to be unpleasant without trying than you could if you worked at it. Unless you have been at sea, you can't realize how infernally miserable it can become. There are a thousand little, insignificant things that can be done to make it miserable. Always something, and it doesn't have to be anything big. Often it is the little things that get under your skin, and the longer it lasts, the worse it gets.

Of course, the food was bad, but that was the steward's fault. Curry and rice and fried potatoes for three straight weeks. That was bad enough, but Duggs kept finding work for us to do after we were off watch. Emergencies, he called them, and you can't refuse duty in an emergency. There were men aboard that ship who would have killed Duggs for a Straits dollar. Me, I'm an easygoing guy, but it was getting to me.

One morning at four o'clock I was coming off watch. It was blowing like the bull of Barney, and a heavy sea running. Duggs had just come on watch, and he calls to me to go aft with him and lend a hand. The log line was fouled. Back we went, and the old tub was rolling her scuppers under, with seas breaking over her that left you gasping like a fish out of water, they were that cold.

We reeled in the log line, hand over hand, the wind tearing at our clothes, the deck awash. He did help some, I'll give him that, but it was me who did the heavy hauling, and it was me who cleared the little propeller on the patent log of seaweed and rope yarns.

Right there was the perfect opportunity. Nobody would have been surprised if we'd both been washed over the side, so it would have been no trick to have dumped him over the rail and washed my hands of him. Duggs had on sea boots and oilskins, and he would have gone down quick.

I finished the job, tearing skin from my hands and getting salt into the raw wounds, the ship plunging like a crazy bronco in a wild and tormented sea. Then, in the moment when I could have got him and got him good, he leaned over and shouted to be heard above the wind, "There! I'm sure glad *I* managed to get that done!"

And I was so mad I forgot to kill him.

The next time was in Port Swettenham. Duggs knew I had a girl in Singapore, but instead of letting me go ashore, he put me on anchor watch. All night long I stood by the rail or walked the deck, looking at the faroff lights of town and cussing the day I shipped on a barge with a louse-bound, scupper-jumping, bilge-swilling rat for mate. And my girl was ashore expecting me —at least, I hoped she was.

We sailed from Singapore, called at Baliwan and Penang, and finally we crawled up the river to Port Swettenham.

It was hot and muggy. Keeping cool was almost impossible, and I had only two changes of clothes for working. One of them I managed to keep clean to wear off watch; the other was stiff with paint and tar. When time allowed I'd wash the one set and switch. The mate deliberately waited one day until I'd changed into clean clothes, and then he called me.

We were taking on some liquid rubber, and down in the empty fuel-oil tank in the forepeak was a spot of water about as big as a pie plate. He told me to climb down fifteen feet of steel ladder covered with oil slime and sop up that water. Aside from being a complete mess before I'd reached the bottom, there was almost an even chance I'd slip and break a leg.

Forward we went together, then down in the forepeak, and stopped by the manhole that let one into the tank. He held up his flashlight, pointing out that dime's worth of water. I had a steel scraper in my hand, and when he leaned over that manhole, I thought what a sweet setup that was.

I could just bend that scraper over his head, drop him into the tank, put the hatch cover on, then go on deck and give them the high sign to start pumping rubber. There'd be a fuss when the mate turned up missing, but they'd never find him until they emptied the tank, and if I knew the old man, I knew he'd never pump the rubber out of that tank for a dozen mates. And just then Chips stuck his head down the hatch and yelled for Duggs.

Time passed, and we tied up in Brooklyn. I drew my pay and walked down the gangway to the dock. Then I turned and looked back.

From beginning to end that voyage had been plain, unadulterated hell, yet I hated to leave. When a guy lives on a ship that long, it begins to feel like home no matter how rough it is, and I had no other.

Six months I'd sailed on that packet, good weather and bad. Around the world we'd gone and in and out of some of the tiniest, dirtiest ports in the Far East. I'd helped to paint her from jack staff to rudder and stood four hours out of every twenty-four at her wheel across three oceans and a half-dozen seas. She was a scummy old barge, but as I stood there looking back, I had to cuss just to keep from feeling bad. Then I walked away.

After that there were other ships and other ports, some good and some bad, but I never forgot Duggs and swore the first time I found him ashore, I'd beat the hell out of him. Every time I'd see that company flag, and they had thirty-odd ships, I'd go hunting for Duggs. I knew that someday I'd find him.

One day in Portland I was walking along with a couple of guys, and I glimpsed that house flag over the top of a warehouse at the dock. Thinks I, now's my chance to get that mug; this will be him.

Sure enough, when I walked down the dock, there he was, giving the last orders before casting off and standing right at the foot of the gangway ready to board. It was now or never. I walked up, all set to cop a Sunday on his chin, and I say, "Remember me?"

He sized me up. "Why, sure! You're Duke, aren't you?" There'd been a time they called me that—among other things.

"That's me. And you—!"

"Well, well!" He was grinning all over. "What do you know about that? We were just talking about you the other day, and we were wondering what had become of you!

"Remember Jones? He's skipper on the *Iron Queen* now, and Edwards—he was third, you'll remember, he's with the Bull Line. They're all scattered now, but that was a good crew, and we came through a lot together. I'll never forget the night you hit that Swede in the Dato Kramat Gardens in Penang! Man, what a wallop that was! I'll bet he's out yet!

"Well," he says then, "I wish we could talk longer. It's like old times to see somebody from the old ship, and we came through, didn't we? We came through some of the roughest weather I ever did see, but we made it! And they say bilge water is thicker than blood. Well, so long, Duke, and good luck!"

Then Duggs stuck out his mitt, and I'll be damned if I didn't shake hands with him!

THE ADMIRAL

Long ago I considered writing an entire book of short stories about Shanghai, but war and revolution changed the situation, leaving it still an important city and one of the great ports of the world but lacking some of the variety and color it formerly possessed.

These next three stories are but little fragments, glimpses that in a small way portray what I had in mind.

AFTER I FINISHED PAINTING the hatch-combing, I walked back aft to the well deck where Tony and Dick were standing by the rail looking down into the Whangpoo. The sampan was there again, and the younger woman was sculling it in closer to the ship's side. When she stopped, the old woman fastened a net on the end of a long stick and held it up to the rail, and Tony put some bread and meat into it.

Every day they came alongside at about the same time, and we were always glad to see them, for we were lonely men. The young woman was standing in the stern as always, and when she smiled, there was something pleasant and agreeable about it that made us feel better. The old woman gave the kids some of the bread and meat, and we stood watching them.

Probably they didn't get meat very often, and bread must have been strange to them, but they ate it very seriously. They were our family, and they seemed to have adopted us just as we adopted them when they first came alongside at Wayside Pier. They had come to ask for "bamboo," which seemed to mean any kind of lumber or wood, and for "chow-chow," which was food, of course. The greatest prize was "soapo," but although most of the Chinese who live like that sell the soap or trade it, our family evidently used it—or some of it.

That was one reason we liked them, one reason they had become our family, because they were clean. They wore the faded blue that all the Chinese of that period seemed to wear, but theirs was always newly washed. We had thrown sticks of dunnage to them or other scrap lumber and some that wasn't scrap, but then the mate came by and made us stop.

There were five of them, the two women and three young ones, living in a sampan. Tony had never seen the like, nor had I, but it was old stuff to Dick, who had been out to the Far East before.

He told us lots of the Chinese lived that way, and some never got ashore from birth to death. There is no room for them on China's crowded soil, so in the seemingly ramshackle boats they grow up, rear families, and die without knowing any other home. There will be a fish net on the roof of the shelter of matting, and on poles beyond the roof the family wash waves in the wind. Sometimes the younger children have buoys fastened to their backs so they will float if they fall over the side.

Two of the children in our family were girls. I have no idea how old they were. Youngsters, anyway. We never saw them any closer than from our rail to the sampan. They were queer little people, images of their mother and the old woman but more serious. Sometimes we'd watch them play by the hour when not working, and they would never smile or laugh. But it was the Admiral who was our favorite. We just called him that because we didn't know his name. He was very short and very serious. Probably he was five years old, but he might have been older or younger. He was a round-faced little tyke, and he regarded us very seriously and maybe a little wistfully, for we were big men, and our ship was high above the water.

We used to give them things. I remember when Tony came back from a spree and brought some chocolate with him. When he was painting over the side on a staging, he dropped it to the Admiral, who was very puzzled. Finally he tasted it and seemed satisfied. After that he tasted everything we dropped to him.

Tony had a red silk handkerchief he thought the world of, but one day he gave it to the Admiral. After that, whenever we saw the Admiral, he was wearing it around his head. But he was still very serious and maybe a little prouder.

Sometimes it used to scare me when I thought of them out there on the Whangpoo in the midst of all that shipping. Partly it was because the Chinese had a bad habit: they would wait till a ship was close by and then cut across her bows real sharp. Dick said they believed they could cut off evil spirits that were following them.

There were wooden eyes painted white with black pupils on either side of the bow of each sampan or junk. They were supposed to watch for rocks or evil spirits. Those eyes used to give me the willies, always staring that way, seeming to bulge in some kind of dumb wonder. I'd wake up at night remembering those eyes and wondering where the Admiral was.

But it got Tony more than me. Tony was a hard guy. He was said to have killed a cop in Baltimore and shipped out to get away. I always thought the old man knew, but he never said anything, and neither did the rest of us. It just wasn't any of our business, and we knew none of the circumstances. Something to do with payoffs, we understood.

Tony took to our family as if they were his own flesh and blood. I never saw a guy get so warmed up over anything. He was a tough wop, and he'd always been a hard case and probably never had anybody he could do for. That's what a guy misses when he's rambling around—not somebody to do something for him but somebody to think of, to work for.

One day when we were working over the side on a staging, the sampan came under us, and Tony turned to wave at the Admiral. "Lookit, Duke," he says to me, "ain't he the cute little devil? That red silk handkerchief sure sets him off."

It was funny, you know? Tony'd been a hard drinker, but after our family showed up, he began to leave it

alone. After he gave that red silk handkerchief to the
Admiral, he just quit drinking entirely, and when the
rest of us went ashore, he'd stay aboard, lying in his
bunk, making something for the Admiral.

Tony could carve. You'd have to see it to believe
how good he was. Of course, in the old days of sail,
men aboard ship carved or created all sorts of things,
working from wood, ivory, or whatever came to hand.
Tony began to carve out a model of our own ship, a
tramp freighter from Wilmington. That was the night
we left for Hong Kong and just a few hours after the
accident.

We had been painting under the stern, hanging there
on a plank staging, and it was a shaky business. The
stern is always the worst place to paint because the
stage is swinging loose underneath, and there isn't a
thing to lay hold of but the ropes at either end.

Worse still, a fellow can't see where the ropes are
made fast to the rail on the poop deck, and those
coolies are the worst guys in the world for untying
every rope they see knotted. One time at Taku Bar I
got dropped into the harbor that way. But this time it
was no trouble like that. It was worse.

We were painting almost overhead when we heard
somebody scream. Both of us turned so quickly we
had to grab the ropes at either end to keep from
falling, and when we got straightened around, we saw
the Admiral in the water.

Our family had been coming toward our ship when
somehow the Admiral had slipped and fallen over the
side, and now there he was, buoyed up by the bladder
fastened to his shoulders, the red handkerchief still on
his head. Probably that had happened a dozen times
before, but this time a big Dollar liner was coming
upstream, and she was right abeam of us when the
Admiral fell. And in a minute more he'd be sucked
down into those whirling propeller blades.

Then the plank jerked from under my feet, and I

fastened to that rope with both hands, and I felt my heart jump with sudden fear. For a minute or so I had no idea what had happened, and by the time I could pull myself up and get my feet on the staging again, Tony was halfway to the Admiral and swimming like I'd seen nobody swim before.

It was nip and tuck, and you can believe it when I say I didn't draw a breath until Tony grabbed the Admiral just as the big liner's stern hove up, the water churning furiously as she was riding high in the water. Tony's head went down, and both he and the Admiral disappeared in the swirl of water that swept out in a wake behind the big liner.

There was a moment there when they were lost in the swirl of water behind the steamer, and then we saw them, and Tony was swimming toward the sampan towing the Admiral, who had both hands on Tony's shoulder.

That night when we slipped down the Whangpoo for Hong Kong, Tony started work on his boat. For we were coming back. We had discharged our cargo and were heading south to pick up more, and by the time we returned, there would be cargo in Shanghai for us.

You'd never guess how much that boat meant to us. All the time we were gone, we thought about our family, and each of us picked up some little thing in Hong Kong or Kowloon to take back to them. But it was the carving of the boat that occupied most of our time. Not that we helped because we didn't. It was Tony's job, and he guarded it jealously, and none of us could have done it half so well.

We watched him carve the amidships house and shape the ventilators, and we craned our necks and watched when he fastened a piece of wire in place as the forestay. When one of us would go on watch, the mate would ask how the boat was coming. Everybody on the ship from the old man to the black cook from

Georgia knew about the ship Tony was carving, and everyone was interested.

Once the chief mate stopped by the fo'c's'le to examine it and offer a suggestion, and the second mate got to telling me about the time his little boy ran his red fire engine into the preacher's foot. Time went by so fast it seemed no time at all till we were steaming back up the Whangpoo again to anchor at Wayside Pier. We were watching for our family long before they could have seen us.

The next morning the boat was finished, and Chips took it down to the paint locker and gave it a coat of paint and varnish, exactly like our own ship; the colors were the same and everything. There wasn't much of a hold, but we had stuffed it with candy. Then we watched for the sampan.

Dick was up on the cross-tree of the mainmast when he saw it, and he came down so fast it was a crying wonder he didn't break a leg. When he hit the deck, he sprinted for the rail. In a few minutes we were all standing there, only nobody was saying anything.

It was the sampan. Only it was bottom up now and all stove in. There wasn't any mistaking it, for we'd have known that particular sampan anywhere even if it hadn't been for the red silk handkerchief. It was there now, a little flag, fluttering gallantly from the wreckage.

SHANGHAI NOT WITHOUT GESTURES

SHE CAME IN from the street and stood watching the auction, a slender girl with great dark eyes and a clear, creamy complexion. It was raining outside on Kiangse Road, and her shoes were wet. From time to time she shifted uncomfortably and glanced about. Once her eyes met mine, and I smiled, but she looked quickly away, watching the auction.

There was always an auction somewhere, it seemed. One day it might be on Range Road or somewhere along the Route Frelupt, tomorrow in Kelmscott Garden. Household effects, usually, for people were always coming or going. The worlds of international business, diplomacy, and the armed services are unstable, and there is much shifting about, from station to station, often without much warning.

I knew none of these people, being an outsider in Shanghai and contented to be so, for a writer, even when a participant, must also be the observer. As yet I was not a writer, only someone wishing to be and endless working toward that end.

There were beautiful things to be seen, Soochow curtains, brass-topped tea tables, intricately carved chests of drawers, even sometimes swords or scimitars with jeweled hilts or the handmade guns of long ago. I used to imagine stories about them and wonder what sort of people had owned them before. It wasn't much of a pastime, but they were dark days, and it was all I could afford.

The girl interested me more. Reading or thinking stories is all right, but living them is better. This girl had obviously not come to buy. She had come to get in out of the rain, to find a place to sit down. Probably it was cold in her rooms.

Rooms? No—more likely just one room, a small place with a few simple things. Some worn slippers, a Japanese silk kimono, and on the old-fashioned dresser would be a picture—a man, of course. He would be an army or naval officer, grave and attractive.

By the way she seemed to be moving her toes inside her shoes and bit her lower lip from time to time, I knew she was tired of walking and her feet were sore.

When I tried to move closer to her, she noticed it and got up to go. I was persistent. There was a story here that I knew well. I had often lived it. When she stepped into the rain, I was beside her.

"Wet, isn't it?" I said, hoping to hear her voice, but she hurried on, turning her face away and ignoring me.

"Please," I said, "I'm not being fresh. I'm just lonely. Weren't you ever lonely?"

She started to walk slower and glanced at me. Her eyes were very dark and even larger than I had thought. She smiled a little, and she had a lovely mouth. "Yes," she said, "I am often lonely."

"Would you like some coffee?" I suggested. "Or tea? What does one drink in Shanghai?"

"Almost everything," she said, and laughed a little. She seemed surprised at the laugh and looked so self-conscious I knew she was hungry. Once you have been very hungry you know the signs in someone else. It makes you feel very different. "But I would like some coffee," she admitted.

We found a little place several blocks away run by a retired French army officer and his wife. We sat down and looked across the table at each other. Her dark suit was a little shabby but neat, and she was obviously tired. I have become sensitive to such things.

There was the slightest bit of an accent in her voice that intrigued me, but I could not place it. I have heard many accents, but I was younger then, and that was the other Shanghai before the guns of Nippon blasted Chapei into smoking ruins and destroyed the fine tempo of the life.

"You are new here?" she asked. "You don't belong here?"

"I have just come," I said, "but I belong nowhere."

"Then you must be at home. Nobody belongs in Shanghai. Everyone is either just going or just arriving."

"You?" I suggested.

She shrugged a shoulder. "I am like you. I belong nowhere. Perhaps Shanghai more than anywhere else because it is a city of passers-by. Not even the Chinese belong here because this city was started for Europeans. It was only a mud flat then."

She moved her feet under the table, and I heard them squish. She had been walking a long time, and her feet were soaked.

"I'm part Russian, but I was born in Nanking. My grandfather left Russia at the time of the Revolution, and for a time they lived in Siberia. There was an order for his arrest, and he escaped over the border with his wife and children. She was French. He met her in Paris when he was a military attaché there.

"I am told he had a little money, but he could never seem to find a place, and the money disappeared. My father was an interpreter in Peking and then in Nanking."

She sipped her coffee, and we ordered sandwiches. This time there was money enough, and for once I had more in prospect. "He knew nothing about the Revolution or the tsar's government and cared less. Everyone talked politics in Peking—all the Russians did, at least. So he came to Nanking where I was born."

"An interesting man. I thought only grand dukes left Russia. What did he do then?"

"My grandfather died and left him whatever there was. For a time we lived very well, and my father drank."

The sandwiches came, and it was several minutes before she touched one, then a small bite only, which she took a long time chewing. I knew the signs, for when one is hungry, it is the taste one wants. In the movies, when they portray a hungry man, he is always gulping down his food, which is entirely false. It is not at all that way, for when one has been truly hungry for some time, the stomach has shrunk, and one can eat but a little at a time. Only in the days after that first meal can one truly eat, and then there is never enough.

"What did he drink?" I asked.

"Fine old Madeira at first. And port. He would sit in the cafes and talk of Tolstoi and Pushkin or of Balzac. He was a great admirer of Balzac. Father had always wished to become a writer, but he only talked of it. He could never seem to sit down and do it."

"There are thousands like him. If one wishes to be a writer, one shouldn't talk about it, one should do it."

"Then he could not afford such wines. He drank vodka then, and finally samshu or Hanskin."

The decline and fall of a refined palate. "And then he died?"

She nodded, but I had known that it had to be. For a man to sink from fine old Madeira to Hanskin—after that there is nothing to do but die.

Our coffee was finished. I looked into the cup, made a mental calculation, and decided against ordering another. "Shall we go?" I suggested.

The rain had resolved itself into a fine mist, and street lights were glowing through the fog that was coming in off the river. It would be this way all night. She hesitated, glanced quickly at me, and held out her hand. "I'd better go."

I took her hand. "Why not come with me? It's going to be an unpleasant night." Her eyes met mine, and she looked quickly away. "Why not?" I said. "It isn't all that much of a place, but it's warm."

"All right," she said.

We walked rapidly. It was not going to be a nasty night; it was already one. A taxi skidded around a corner throwing a shower of spray that only just missed us. A rickshaw passed, going the other way, its curtains drawn. I was glad when we reached the door.

For myself it did not matter. Sometimes I walked for hours in the rain, but she was not dressed warm, and the rain was cold and miserable. The Shanghai streets were not a place to be at night and alone.

My place was warm. My boy was gone. I called him my "number-only" boy. I told him when he took the job he couldn't be the "number-one" boy because there would not be a number two, three, or four.

It was not just a room but a small apartment, pleasant in a way. Drifting men have a way of fixing up almost any place they stop to make it comfortable. Seamen often fix things up like any old maid might do and for much the same reason.

Yet the apartment was not mine. I'd been given the use of it by a Britisher who was up country now. His name was Haig, and he came and went a good deal with no visible means of support, and I was told that he often stayed up country months at a time. He had been an officer in one of the Scottish regiments, I believe. I had a suspicion that he was still involved in some kind of duty, although he had many weird Asiatic connections.

Some of the books were mine, and it pleased me

when she went to the books immediately. It always makes a sucker out of a man who truly loves books to see someone taking a genuine interest in them.

Later, when she came out of the shower wearing my robe, her eyes were very bright. I hadn't realized she was so pretty. We sat by the fire, watching the coals.

"Lose your job?" I asked finally.

"Two weeks ago, and it came at a bad time. My rent was up last week, and there is always a demand for lodgings here. This morning they said not to come back unless I could pay."

"That's tough. What's your line?"

"I've done a lot of things. A secretary, usually. I can handle five languages very well and two others a little. I worked for Moran and Company in Tientsin, and then here for a transport firm, but lately there has been so little business, and the owner has been gambling. I don't know what I'm going to do."

Outside was China. Outside was Shanghai, the old Shanghai when it was an international city. Outside were the millions, of all nationalities. French, English, Japanese, Dutch, German, Sikh, Portuguese, Hebrew, Greek, Malay, and of course, Chinese. Outside was the Whangpoo, a dark river flowing out of China, out of old China and into the new, then down to the sea. Outside rivers of men flowed along the dark streets, men buying and selling, men fighting and gambling, men bargaining and selling, loving and dying. Millions of men, women, and children, opening countless doors, going into lives of which I knew nothing, eating the food of many countries, speaking in tongues I had never heard, praying to many gods.

Listening to her as she spoke of China, I remembered the shuffle of feet in the noontime streets. There was nothing I could do. It was bad for a man to be broke but so much worse for a woman. Especially for such a girl as this.

Perhaps I was a fool, but I, too, had been hungry. Soon there would be a ship, and I would go to Bombay or Liverpool or New York, while she—

"You wouldn't have come had there been any other place to go, would you?"

"No."

A lock of her dark hair had fallen against my robe. It looked good there. So black against the soft white of her throat.

"But I am grateful. What could I have done?"

"Well, what? I had a feeling I was going to make a fool of myself. Americans are a sentimental lot, and every cynic is a sentimentalist under the skin. I knew enough about women to be skeptical but had been hungry enough to be human.

A wind moaned about the eaves, and rain dashed against the window.

"Listen," I said, "this isn't quite the sporting thing, is it? To have you come here because there was nowhere else to go and because I bought you a cup of coffee? Or maybe because of breakfast in the morning? I don't like the sound of it.

"Well, hell, I'm going to sleep on the sofa, and you can have the other room."

After the door closed, I stood looking at it. If she hadn't been so damned lovely it would have been easier to be gallant. Probably right now she was thinking what a sap I was. Well, she wouldn't be the only one.

I had a feeling I was going to be sorry for this in the morning.

THE MAN WHO STOLE SHAKESPEARE

WHEN I HAD BEEN in Shanghai but a few days, I rented an apartment in a narrow street off Avenue Edward VII where the rent was surprisingly low. The door at the foot of the stairs opened on the street beside a moneychanger's stall, an inconspicuous place that one might pass a dozen times a day and never notice.

At night I would go down into the streets and wander about or sit by my window and watch people going about their varied business. From my corner windows I could watch a street intersection and an alleyway, and there were many curious things to see, and for one who finds his fellow man interesting, there was much to learn.

Late one afternoon when a drizzle of despondent rain had blown in from the sea, I decided to go out for coffee. Before reaching my destination, it began to pour, so I stepped into a bookstore for shelter.

This store dealt in secondhand books published in several languages and was a jumble of stacks, piles, and racks filled with books one never saw elsewhere and was unlikely to see again. I was hitch reading from Sterne when I saw him.

He was a small man and faded. His face had the scholarly expression that seems to come from familiarity with books, and he handled them tenderly. One could see at a glance that here was a man who knew a good book when he saw one, with a feeling for attractive format as well as content.

Yet when I glanced up, he was slipping a book into his pocket. Quickly, with almost a sense of personal guilt, I looked toward the clerk, but he was watching the rain. The theft had passed unobserved.

Now there is a sort of sympathy among those who love books, an understanding that knows no bounds of race, creed, or financial rating. If a man steals a necktie, he is a thief of the worst stripe. If he steals a car, nothing is too bad for him. But a man who steals a book is something else—unless it is my book.

My first thought when he slipped the book into his pocket was to wonder what book he wanted badly enough to steal. Not that there are only a few books worth stealing, for there are many. Yet I was curious. What, at the moment, had captured his interest? This small, gentle-seeming man with the frayed shirt collar and the worn topcoat?

When he left, I walked over to the place where the book had been and tried to recall what it might have been, for I had only just checked that shelf myself. Then I remembered.

It had been a slim, one-play-to-the-volume edition of Shakespeare. He had also examined Hakluyt's *Voyages,* or at least one volume of the set, Huysmans' *Against the Grain,* and Burton's *Anatomy of Melancholy*.

This was definitely a man I wished to know. Also, I was curious. Which play had he stolen? Was it the play itself he wished to read? Or was it for some particular passage in the play? Or to complete a set?

Turning quickly, I went to the door, and barely in time. My man was just disappearing in the direction of Thibet Road, and I started after him, hurrying.

At that, I almost missed him. He was just rounding a corner a block away, so he had been running, too. Was it the rain or a feeling of guilt?

The rain had faded into a drizzle once more. My man kept on, walking rapidly, but fortunately for me, he was both older than I, and his legs were not as long.

Whether he saw me, I do not know, but he led me a lively chase. It seemed scarcely possible for a man to go up and down so many streets, and he obviously knew Shanghai better than I. Yet suddenly he turned into an alley and dodged down a basement stairway. Following him, I got my foot in the door before he could close it.

He was frightened, and I could understand why. In those wilder years they found several thousand bodies on the street every year, and he perhaps had visions of adding his own to the list. Being slightly over six feet and broad in the shoulder, I must have looked dangerous in that dark passageway. Possibly he had visions of being found in the cold light of dawn with a slit throat, for such things were a common occurrence in Shanghai.

"Here!" he protested. "You can't do this!" That I was doing it must have been obvious. "I'll call an officer!"

"And have to explain that volume of Shakespeare in your pocket?" I suggested.

That took the wind out of him, and he backed into the room, a neat enough place, sparsely furnished except for the books. The walls were lined with them.

"Now see here," I said, "you've nothing to worry about. I don't intend to report you, and I'm not going to rob you. I'm simply interested in books and in the books people want enough to steal.

"You're not from the book store?"

"Nothing of the kind. I saw you slip the book into

your pocket, and although I did not approve, I was
curious as to what you had stolen and why." I held out
my hand. "May I see?"

He shook his head, then stood back and watched
me, finally taking off his coat. He handed me the book
from his pocket, which was a copy of *Henry IV*, bound
in gray cloth with a thin gold line around the edges. The
book was almost new and felt good to the hands. I
turned the pages, reading a line or two. "You've a lot
of books," I said, glancing at the shelves. "May I
look?"

He nodded, then stepped back and sat down. He
certainly was not at ease, and I didn't blame him.

The first book I saw was Wells's *Outline of History*.
"Everybody has that one," I commented.

"Yes," he said hesitantly.

Ibsen was there, and Strindberg, Chekhov, and Tolstoi. A couple of volumes by Thomas Hardy were
wedged alongside three by Dostoevsky. There were
books by Voltaire, Cervantes, Carlyle, Goldoni, Byron,
Verlaine, Baudelaire, Cabell, and Hume.

The next book stopped me short, and I had to look
again to make sure the bookshelf wasn't kidding. It
was a quaint, old-fashioned, long-out-of-date *Home
Medical Advisor* by some Dr. Felix Peabody, published by some long-extinct publisher whose state of
mind must have been curious, indeed.

"Where in the world did you get this?" I asked. "It
seems out of place stuck in between Hegel and Hud-
son."

He smiled oddly, his eyes flickering to mine and
then away. He looked nervous, and since then I have
often wondered what he must have been thinking and
what went through his mind at that moment.

Scanning the shelves to take stock of what his interests were, I came upon another queer one. It was
between Laurence Sterne's *Sentimental Journey* and

George Gissing's *Private Papers of Henry Ryecroft*. It was *Elsie's Girlhood*.

After that I had to sit down. This man was definitely some kind of a nut. I glanced at him, and he squirmed a little. Evidently he had seen my surprise at the placement of some of the books or the fact that he had them at all.

"You must read a lot," I suggested. "You've a lot of good books here."

"Yes," he said; then he leaned forward, suddenly eager to talk. "It's nice to have them. I just like to own them, to take them in my hands and turn them over and to know that so much that these men felt, saw, thought, and understood is here. It is almost like knowing the men themselves."

"It might be better," I said. "Some of these men were pretty miserable in themselves, but their work is magnificent."

He started to rise, then sat down again suddenly as though he expected me to order him to stay where he was.

"Do you read a lot?" he asked.

"All the time," I said. "Maybe even too much. At least when I have books or access to them."

"My eyes"—he passed a hand over them—"I'm having trouble with my glasses. I wonder if you'd read to me sometime? That is," he added hastily "if you have the time."

"That's the one thing I've plenty of," I said. "At least until I catch a ship. Sure I'll read to you."

As a matter of fact, he had books here of which I'd heard all my life but had found no chance to read. "If you want, I'll read some right now."

It was raining outside, and I was blocks from my small apartment. He made coffee, and I read to him, starting with *The Return of the Native* for no reason other than that I'd not read it and it was close at hand.

Then I read a bit from *Tales of Mean Streets* and some from Locke's *Essay Concerning Human Understanding.*

Nearly every day after that I went to see Mr. Meacham. How he made his living, I never knew. He had some connection, I believe, with one of the old trading companies, for he seemed very familiar with the interior of China and with people there.

The oddity of it appealed to some irony in my sense of humor. A few weeks before I'd been coiling wet lines on the forecastle head of a tramp steamer, and now here I was, reading to this quaint old gentleman in his ill-fitting suit.

He possessed an insatiable curiosity about the lives of the authors and questioned me about them by the hour. That puzzled me, for a reader just naturally acquires some such knowledge just by reading the bookjackets, and in the natural course of events a man can learn a good deal about the personal lives of authors. However, he seemed to know nothing about them and was avid for detail.

There was much about him that disturbed me. He was so obviously alone, seemingly cut off from everything. He wasn't bold enough to make friends, and there seemed to be no reason why anybody should take the trouble to know him. He talked very little, and I never did know where he had come from or how he happened to be in such a place as Shanghai, for he was a contradiction to everything one thinks of when one considers Shanghai. You could imagine him in Pittsburgh, St. Louis, or London, in Glasgow or Peoria, but never in such a place as this.

One day when I came in, I said, "Well, you name it. What shall I read today?"

He hesitated, flushed, then took a book from the shelf and handed it to me. It was *Elsie's Girlhood,* a book of advice to a young girl about to become a woman.

For a minute I thought he was kidding, and then I was sure it couldn't be anything else. "Not today," I said. "I'll try Leacock."

When I remembered it afterward, I remembered he had not seemed to be kidding. He had been perfectly serious and obviously embarrassed when I put him off so abruptly. He hesitated, then put the book away, and when I returned the next day, the book was no longer on the shelf. It had disappeared.

It was that day that I guessed his secret. I was reading at the time, and it just hit me all of a sudden. It left me completely flabbergasted, and for a moment I stared at the printed page from which I was reading, my mouth open for words that would not come.

Yes, I told myself, that had to be it. There was no other solution. All the pieces suddenly fell into place, the books scattered together without plan or style, with here and there books that seemed so totally out of place and unrelated.

That night I read later than ever before.

Then I got a job. Dou Yu-seng offered to keep the rent paid on my apartment (I always suspected he owned the building) while I took care of a little job up the river. I knew but little about him but enough to know of affiliations with various war lords and at least one secret society. However, what I was to do was legitimate.

Yet when I left, I kept thinking of old Mr. Meacham. He would be alone again, with nobody to read to him.

Alone? Remembering those walls lined with books, I knew he would never actually be alone. They were books bought here and there, books given him by people moving away, books taken from junk heaps, but each one of them represented a life, somebody's dream, somebody's hope or idea, and all were there where he could touch them, feel them, know their presence.

No, he would not be alone, for he would remember Ivan Karamazov, who did not want millions but an answer to his questions. He would remember those others who would people his memories and walk through the shadows of his rooms: *Jean Valjean, Julien Sorel, Mr. John Oakhurst,* gambler, and, of course, the little man who was *the friend of Napoleon.*

He knew line after line from the plays and sonnets of Shakespeare and a lot of Keats, Kipling, Li Po, and *Kasidah.* He would never really be alone now.

He never guessed that I knew, and probably for years he had hidden his secret, ashamed to let anyone know that he, who was nearly seventy and who so loved knowledge, had never learned to read.

A FRIEND OF THE GENERAL

They knew each other by name and sometimes
by sight. Occasionally those who were in the
city would have a drink together at the Astor
Bar or a lesser known place, off the beaten
track, called the International. In the years from
1920 until the beginning of World War II it was
the place to which they came. The war lords
were hiring men who had specialties, although
it was the flyers who were most in demand.
Some of their names became legend: some were
never known but to each other and those who
hired them. There were others who never came
to Shanghai but whose names were known, for
they were men of a kind. One-Arm Sutton,
General Rafael de Nogales, Joseph Trebitsch-
Lincoln, and, of course, their long-dead prede-
cessor, Gen. Frederick Townsend Ward, commander of the "Ever-Victorious Army" to whom
the Chinese raised a statue.

They were soldiers of fortune, men who made
their living by their knowledge of weapons and
tactics, selling their services wherever there was
a war.

The munitions dealers were there, also, mingling
with diplomats and officers of a dozen armies
and navies. Thirteen flags, it was said, floated
over Shanghai, but there were always visiting
naval vessels from still other countries.

The terrorist tactics that have become so much
a part of world news in these later years were
an old story in Shanghai. Korean, Chinese, and

Japanese gunmen killed each other with impunity, and if one was discreet, one avoided the places where these affairs were most likely to take place. There were a few places frequented by each group, and unless one enjoyed lead with one's meals, it was wise to go elsewhere. The Carlton, fortunately, was not one of these places, and they had boxing matches as part of the floor show. A fighter who did not become too destructive too soon could make a decent living there and at a few other spots. The secret was to win, if one could, but not so decisively as to frighten possible opponents, for there were not too many fighters available.

When I first met the general, I had no memory of him, but a chance remark brought it all back. He had been a regular, always sitting close to the ring and giving the fights his full attention. My time in Shanghai was too brief to really know the place, although some of my friends knew it about as well as one could. From them I learned a great deal, and with some small skill I had for observing what goes on, I learned more.

I T BEGAN QUITE CASUALLY as such things often do, with a group of people conversing about nothing in particular, all unsuspecting of what the result might be.

My company was quartered in the chateau of the countess, as during the war she had moved into what had once been the gardener's cottage. It was the sort of place that in Beverly Hills would have sold well into six figures, a warm, cozy place with huge fireplaces, thick walls, and flowers all about.

The countess was young, very beautiful, and clever. She had friends everywhere and knew a bit of what went on anywhere you would care to mention. I was there because of the countess, and so, I suppose, was everybody else.

Her sister had just come down from the Netherlands, their first visit since the German occupation. There was a young American naval attaché, a woman of indeterminate age who was a Russian émigré, a fragile blond actress from Paris who, during the war, had smuggled explosives hidden under the vegetables in a basket on her bicycle. There was a baron who wore his monocle as if it were a part of him but had no other discernible talents and an American major who wanted to go home.

The war was fizzling out somewhere in Germany, far from us, and I wondered aloud where in Paris one could find a decent meal.

They assured me this was impossible unless I knew a good black-market restaurant. Due to the war there was a shortage of everything, and the black-market cafes had sprung up like speakeasies during the Prohibition era in the States—and like them you had to know somebody to get in.

Each had a different restaurant to suggest, although there was some agreement on one or two, but the countess solved my dilemma. Tearing a bit of note paper from a pad, she wrote an address. "Go to this place. Take a seat in a corner away from the windows, and when you wish to order, simply tell the waiter you are a friend of the general."

"But who," somebody asked, "is the general?"

She ignored the question but replied to mine when I asked, "But suppose the general is there at the time?"

"He will not be. He has flown to Baghdad and will go from there to Chabrang."

I could not believe that I had heard right.

"To *where?*" the naval attaché asked.

"It is a small village," I said, "near the ruins of Tsaparang."

"Now," the Russian woman said, "we understand everything! Tsaparang! Of course! Who would not know Tsaparang?"

"Where," the naval attaché asked, "are the ruins of Tsaparang?"

"Once," I began, "there was a kingdom—"

"Don't bother him with that. If I know Archie, he will waste the next three weeks trying to find it on a map."

"Take this"—she handed me the address—"and do as I have said. You will have as fine a meal as there is in Paris, as there is in Europe, in fact."

"But how can they do it?" Jeannine asked. "How can any cafe—"

"It is not the restaurant," the countess said, "it is the general. Before the war began, he knew it was coming, and he prepared for it. He has his own channels of communication, and being the kind of man he is, they work, war or no war.

"During a war some people want information, others want weapons or a way to smuggle escaped prisoners, but the general wanted the very best in food and wine, but above all, condiments, and he had them."

The general, it seemed, had served his apprenticeship during Latin American revolutions, moving from there to the Near and Middle East, to North Africa, and to China. Along the way he seemed to have feathered his nest quite substantially.

A few days later, leaving my jeep parked in a narrow street, I went through a passage between buildings and found myself in a small court. There were several shops with artists' studios above them, and in a corner under an awning were six tables. Several workmen sat at one table drinking beer. At another was a young man, perhaps a student, sitting over his books and a cup of coffee.

Inside the restaurant it was shadowed and cool. The floor was flagstone, and the windows hung with curtains. Everything was painfully neat. There were cloths on the tables and napkins. Along one side there was a bar with several stools. There were exactly twelve tables, and I had started for the one in the corner when a waiter appeared.

He indicated a table at one side. "Would you sit here, please?"

My uniform was, of course, American. That he spoke English was not unusual. Crossing to the table, I sat down with my back to the wall, facing the court. The table in the corner was but a short distance away and was no different from the others except that in the immediate corner there was a very large, comfortable chair with arms, not unlike what is commonly called a captain's chair.

"You wished to order?"

"I do." I glanced up. "I am a friend of the general."

"Ah? Oh, yes! Of course."

Nothing more was said, but the meal served was magnificent. I might even say it was unique.

A few days later, being in the vicinity, I returned, and then a third time. On this occasion I was scarcely seated when I heard footsteps in the court; looking up, I found the door darkened by one who could only be the general.

He was not tall, and he was—corpulent. He was neatly dressed in a tailored gray suit with several ribbons indicative of decorations. The waiter appeared at once, and there was a moment of whispered conversation during which he glanced at me.

Embarrassed? Of course. Here I had been passing myself as this man's friend, obtaining excellent meals under false pretenses. That I had paid for them and paid well made no difference at all. I had presumed, something no gentleman would do.

He crossed to his table and seated himself in his captain's chair. He ordered Madeira, and then the waiter crossed to my table. "Lieutenant? The general requests your company. He invites you to join him."

A moment I hesitated, then rising, I crossed over to him. "General? I must apolo—"

"Please be seated." He gestured to a chair.

"But I must—"

"You must do nothing of the kind. Have they taught you nothing in that army of yours? Never make excuses. Do what has to be done, and if it fails, accept the consequences."

"Very well." I seated myself. "I shall accept the consequences."

"Which will be an excellent meal, some very fine wine, and I hope some conversation worthy of the food and the wine." He glanced at me. "At least you are soldier enough for that. To find a very fine meal and take advantage of it. A soldier who cannot feed himself it no soldier at all."

He filled my glass, then his. "One question. How did you find this place? Who told you of me?"

Of course, I could have lied, but he would see through it at once. I disliked bringing her into it but knew that under the circumstances she would not mind.

"It was," I said, "the countess—"

"Of course," he interrupted me. "Only she would have dared." He glanced at me. "You know her well?"

It was nobody's business how well I knew her. "We are friends. My company is quartered in her chateau, and she is a lovely lady."

"Ah? How pleasant for you. She is excellent company, and such company is hard to come by these days. A truly beautiful woman, but clever. Altogether too clever for my taste. I do not trust clever women."

"I rather like them."

"Ah, yes. But you are a lieutenant. When you are a general, you will feel otherwise."

He spent a good deal of time watching the court, all of which was visible from where he sat. He had chosen well. The court had but one entrance for the public, although for the fortunate ones who lived close there were no exits, as I later discovered.

Not only could he not be approached from behind, but anyone emerging from the passage was immediately visible to him, while they could not see him until they actually entered the restaurant.

On our second meeting I surprised him and put myself in a doubtful position. I was simply curious, and my question had no other intent.

"How did you like Chabrang?"

He had started to lift his glass, and he put it down immediately. His right hand slid to the edge of the table until only his fingertips rested there. His tone was distinctly unfriendly when he replied, "What do you mean?"

"When I asked the countess if you would be here, she said you were in Baghdad—on the way to Chabrang."

"She said *that?* She mentioned Chabrang?"

"Yes, and I was surprised. It isn't the sort of place people hear of, being in such an out-of-the-way place, and only a village—a sort of way station."

His right hand dropped into his lap, and his fingers tugged at his trouser leg, which clung a bit too snugly to his heavy thigh. "You know Chabrang."

It was not a question but a statement. His right hand hitched the pant leg again. Suddenly I realized what was on his mind, and I almost laughed, for I'd been away from that sort of thing too long and had become careless. The laugh was not for him but simply that it seemed like old times, and it was kind of good to be back.

"You won't need the knife," I told him. "I am no danger to you."

"You know Chabrang, and there are not fifty men in Europe who know it. Am I to believe this is pure coincidence?"

He had a knife in his boot top, I was sure of that. He was a careful man and no doubt had reason to be, but why that was so I had no idea and told him as much.

"It was my only way out," he said. "They found me, but they were looking for a man who was carrying a great lot of money, and I had nothing but food, weapons, and some butterflies. They let me go."

"I believed it was a way out for me, too," I said, "but I was not so lucky. I had to turn back."

He turned to look at me. "When were you in China?"

"It was long ago." I have never liked dates. Perhaps because I have a poor memory for dates in my own life. "It was in the time of the war lords," I said.

He shrugged. "That's indefinite enough."

We talked of many things. He gestured widely. "This is what I wanted," he said. "I wanted time— leisure. Time to read, to think, to see. Some people make it some ways, some another. Mine was through war."

"It is no longer regarded with favor," I suggested.

He shrugged again. "Who cares? For ten thousand years it was the acceptable way for a man to make his fortune. A young man with a strong arm and some luck could go off to the wars and become rich.

"All the old kingdoms were established so. All the original 'great families' were founded in just such a way. What else was William the Conqueror? Or Roger of Sicily? Or their Viking ancestors who first con- quered and then settled in Normandy? What does Norman mean but Northmen? Who were Cortés and Pizarro? They were young men with swords."

"Ours is a different world," I suggested. "Our stan- dards are not the same."

"Bah!" He waved his fork. "The standards are the same, only now the fighting is done by lawyers. There is more cunning and less courage. They will sell you the arms—"

"Like Milton," I said.

He stopped with his fork in the air and his mouth open. "You know about Milton," he said. "I am be- ginning to wonder about you, lieutenant."

"Everybody in China knew that story. Perhaps I should say everybody in our line of business or around the Astor Bar. It was no secret."

"Perhaps not. Perhaps not."

Such stories are repeated in bars and tearooms, over bridge tables as well as in the waterfront dives. Milton had been a well set up man in his early forties, as I recall him. A smooth, easy-talking man, somewhat florid of face, who played a good game of golf, haunt- ed the Jockey Club, and owned a few good racehorses, Mongolian ponies brought down for that purpose. He had been a dealer in guns, supplying the various war lords with rifles, machine guns, mortars, and ammunition. As a machine gun was worth its weight in gold and as some European nation was always liquidating its stores to replace them with more modern weapons, Milton did well.

He reminded me of a first-class insurance salesman, and in a sense that was what he was. The weapons he sold were the kind of insurance they needed.

He might have become enormously wealthy, but he had an urge to gamble, and he had a blonde. The blonde, some said, was none too bright, but she had other assets that were uniquely visible, and nobody really inquired as to her intelligence, least of all Milton.

A day came when too much blonde and too much gambling left him nearly broke, and she chose that moment to say she wanted to go to Paris. She pleaded, she argued, and he listened. He was willing enough, but the problem was money.

At that moment an order came for six thousand rifles, some machine guns and mortars, with ammunition for all. Milton had only six hundred rifles on hand and insufficient cash. Such deals were always cash on the barrel head. He agreed to supply what was needed.

Long ago he had arranged a little deal with the customs officials to pass anything he shipped in a piano box, and as a piano salesman he seemed to be doing very well indeed.

Knowing the kind of people with whom he dealt, he also knew the necessity for absolute secrecy in what he was about to do, so with one German whom he knew from long experience would not talk, he went to his warehouse, and locking the doors very carefully, he proceeded to pack the cases with old, rusted pipe and straw. Atop each case, before closing it, he put a few rifles to satisfy any quick inspection. Yet the greatest thing he had going for him was his reputation for integrity. He supervised the loading of the piano boxes on a Chinese junk and collected his down payment of three hundred thousand dollars.

He had taken every precaution. Through a close-mouthed acquaintance he had bought two tickets on a vessel that was sailing that very night.

"Pack an overnight bag for each of us," he said. "Nothing more. And be ready. Say nothing to anyone and I'll buy you a completely new wardrobe in Paris."

Now, his rifles loaded on the junk, he drove at once to his apartment on Bubbling Well Road. He ran lightly up the steps carrying the small black bag. "Come! We've got to move fast! There's not much time to catch the boat!"

This, you must remember, was before World War II, and there were no airlines as such.

"Where are the tickets?" he asked.

She came to him, her blue eyes wide and wonderful. "Oh, Milt! I hope you're not going to be angry, but the Funstons are having a party tonight, and they are always such *fun!* Well, I turned in our tickets and got tickets on another boat, a much faster one, that leaves tomorrow!"

No doubt there was a moment of sheer panic: then what he hoped was common sense prevailed. It would take that junk a week to get to its destination. Well—four days at least. There was nothing to be done, and why not one more night?

The next morning was one I would never forget. I'd known Milton only to speak to, although we did have a drink together once. When a friend banged on my door at daybreak and told me he had something to show me, I went along.

What he showed me was what Milton might have expected, for the men with whom he did business did not play games.

There, standing upright in the parking lot outside his place on Bubbling Well Road, was a piece of the rusty pipe he had so carefully packed. On top of it was Milton's head. His complexion was no longer florid.

"Everybody knew that story," I repeated. "At least everybody of our sort. I heard it again a few days ago in the Casual Officers' Mess on Place St. Augustine."

"But you know about Chabrang," the general said.

The wine was excellent. "I see no connection," I said.

He gave me a sidelong glance, filled with suspicion. Why the mention of Chabrang disturbed him, I could not guess, as it was but an unimportant village on one of the routes out of Sinkiang to Ladakh. It was in no way noteworthy except that it was near the ruins of Tsaparang. The ruins represented about all that remained of a long-ago kingdom.

"Did you know Milton?" I asked.

"I knew him. If the Chinese had not killed him, I would have. Those munitions were consigned to me."

"To *you?*"

"They were consigned to me for the war lord, and the fraud put my head on the block. I was suspected of complicity."

"What happened?"

"I acted. Perceiving that I was suspected, and knowing the gentleman concerned was not one to dilly-dally, I made my move. You see, he already owed me money, a considerable sum. By disposing of me, he could make somebody atone for the fraud and liquidate his debt at the same time."

He fell silent while the waiter brought a steaming platter of seafood. When he had gone, the general resumed. "It was the time to move, so I acted. Remember that this is the first principle—*act!* Remember that, my young friend! Do not deliberate! Do not hesitate! Do not wait upon eventuality! *Act!* It is always better to do something, even if not quite the right thing, than to do nothing. *Action! Decision!* Only these are important!"

He toyed with an oyster, glancing from under his brows. "My mind, at such times, works quickly. He needed a scapegoat to save face. Not in Shanghai but there, before his men! At once! Instantly I perceived it was I who must pay."

He ate the oyster, and taking a bit of bread, buttered it lavishly. Many of the good people of France had not seen so much butter in months.

"You see, the commander himself did not yet know of the fraud, but immediately the discovery was made, an officer had left to report to him. He could reach him in not less than an hour, then an hour to return.

"The captain of the junk had seen none of what went on, so I went to him immediately, put money in his hand, and told him to sail to such and such a point up river. The cargo would be received there.

"Then I went to the telegraph station, which was closed. I broke into it and sent a message to another, rival war lord up the river, offering the guns to him for a fancy price. He was desperately in need of them, and I told him I could promise delivery if the money was paid to me in gold. A place of payment was mentioned.

"There was a charter plane at the field. You knew him, I think? Milligan? He would fly you anywhere for a price and land his plane on a pocket handkerchief if need be. Moreover, he could be trusted, and there were some, in those days, who could not. I placed five hundred dollars in his hand and said I wished to leave for Shanghai at once.

" 'After I gas up,' he said.

" 'Now,' I told him. 'Right now. There is petrol at—' I took his map and put my finger on the place. 'And you can land there.'

" 'If you say so,' he replied doubtfully. 'I never heard of—'

" 'The petrol is there,' I promised him. 'I had it placed there for just such an emergency.' "

The general looked around at me. "You are young, lieutenant, and wise as you may be, you are still learning, so remember to trust no one! Prepare for every eventuality no matter how remote! Not even a mouse trusts himself to one hole only. That is an old saying, but it has remained in my mind, and can I be less wise than a mouse?

"We took off at once. Within twenty minutes of my realization I *acted!* And that night I was in Shanghai with *her!*"

"Her?" He had lost me.

"Of course! With Milton's blonde. What was her name? I've forgotten. No matter. I was there, consoling her.

"Of course"—he glanced at me—"I was younger then and not so—so—well, I am a little overweight now. But then, ah, I was handsome then, lieutenant! I was handsome, and I was, of course, younger.

"I found her in tears. She was weeping for him. For Milton. Or perhaps she was weeping for that lost trip to Paris. About women, lieutenant, one never knows. No matter.

"There on the floor was the black bag. It was out of the way, back against the sofa's end, but I recognized it at once. True, I'd never seen it before, but I'd seen others of the kind. In it would be the money! All that delightful, beautiful money! And she was crying? Well, as I have said, she was a woman, and about women one never knows.

"I consoled her. What else could I do? What does one do with a pretty woman who is sad and has a quarter of a million dollars, give or take a few? I told her she must not worry, that I—*I* would take her to Paris! And who knew Paris better? Who knew the night spots, the cafes, the bordel— Well, who knew the town better than I? Even its history!

"Oh, I was marvelous that day! I told her exciting and glamorous tales of what the city was like, of living there, and I dropped names, names of all the famous and infamous. As a matter of fact, I actually did know some of them.

"She was consoled! She rested her head on my shoulder. As you have seen, they are very broad. She dried her tears; then she smoothed her dress, she touched up her makeup, and she said, 'I still have the tickets. We could go at once. I—there is nothing more for me here! Nothing!'

" 'I know.' I took her two hands. 'It is tragic. But in Paris, my dear, you can forget. In Paris there is music, there is dancing, there is love, and there is beauty! And we shall be there—together!' "

He paused, refilling his glass. "She listened, her blue eyes very wide and wondering. She was a dear girl, no question of it. The black bag was at my feet. 'Look!' I took from my pocket a packet of bills and stripped off several of the thousand-dollar denomination. 'Take this! I shall meet you in Paris! Go to this place—' I wrote out the name of a small, discreet hotel—'and wait for me. I shall not be long.'

"Then I picked up the black bag and walked out. Once beyond the door with the bag I did not wait for the lift, but ran down the stairs. I had it, did I not? I had the black bag with the quarter of a million, and more to come from my own sale of the munitions! Ah, it was exciting, my friend, most exciting! It is always exciting when one is making money! And such delightful sums! Into my car then and away to the field where Milligan awaited me.

"Racing out on the field, I leaped from the car. Milligan was there, beside his plane, but he was not alone.

"Three men were with him, and one of them was the old marshal. He was the last person I expected in Shanghai, where he had many enemies, but here he was. One of the men stood guard over Milligan, and the other had a pistol directed at me."

"My eyes caught those of Milligan. He was a man I knew—a tough man, a ready man. Did I tell you that he was from Texas? Anyway, a lift of the brows, a small hand gesture—he knew what was coming. There was no doubting that he wished to be away as much as I.

" 'Ah, marshall Chang! How delightful to see you! And what a surprise to find you in Shanghai of all places! Once I knew what happened I flew here at once! At once, marshal! It was my duty as your aide, your confidant, and your friend to rectify this error!'

"You see, one does what one can, and I had already given up on this money. True, what I was about to do would *hurt!* Hurt, lieutenant! But it was my only way out. The old marshal would be in no mood for games, and every second here was filled with danger for him, so he was desperate. As for me, it is a wise soldier who knows when to retire from the field.

"Anyway, did I not have money awaiting me at the other end? From my sale of the arms?

" 'When I realized what had happened, marshal, I flew to recover your money! It was the least I could do for one who has been my friend, my adviser, almost a second father!'

" 'Recover?' he asked, puzzled.

" 'Of course! It is here! In this bag! Now if you would like to fly back with me?'

" 'Let me see the money,' he demanded.

" 'Of course,' I said, and yielded the bag to his grasp. Yielded it reluctantly, you understand, for I had hoped to have that money somehow, someway. If I could just get the marshal into the plane—

"He gestured to one of his men, he who had been covering me, to open the bag. He did so. The marshal leaned over and peered inside; then he looked up at me, and his face was dark with anger.

"Looking into the bag, I knew why, knew that we had been cheated, that—

"The bag was filled with old newspapers, and there was a novel there to give it weight. And *that* novel? How could it have had weight enough? It was by a writer I have never liked—never!

"The old marshal was trembling with anger. 'You!' he shouted. 'You—!'

"It was a time, lieutenant, a time for decision! Never have I been more pleased with myself than what I did then! In an instant I should have been killed! And Milligan, also! It was a time for *action*, and like the old soldier I was, I *acted!*

"He who guarded me had lowered his pistol while he opened the bag, and for that reason he was holding the pistol but loosely. I struck down at the base of his thumb with the edge of my hand, and as the pistol fell from his hand, I seized it and fired!

"Not at the man I had disarmed but at the man guarding Milligan.

"Turning swiftly, I shoved the old marshal. He was a heavy man, and he tottered back off balance and fell. Milligan had leaped into the plane, and the man I had disarmed leaped at me. My pistol exploded, and he fell; then I leaped into the plane, and we were off— gone!

"Once again, lieutenant, I had snatched victory from the jaws of defeat. I do not wish to appear smug, but it is only the truth.

"In Kansu I received payment for the guns and told them where the junk would be. Then once more we took off. In the air I changed clothing, changed to such a costume as an English scientist might wear in the field. I had it always with me, for you know how the English are—one is apt to find them anywhere, in any out of the way, godforsaken place, doing God knows what.

"I was to be a hunter of butterflies and a bit vague about all else. You see? It was an excellent cover.

"We landed—I shall not say where, for it is a field I have often used and may well use again. I have such places here and there. One never knows, does one?

"There I paid Milligan. Ten thousand dollars, more than he had ever seen before at one time, and there I left him, but with regret. He was a man, that one!

"I bought horses, and in a small town I found some equipment abandoned at some time by a scientific scholar before he attempted the Karakoram Pass. Have you tried it? If not, do not. It is—anyway, there is another older pass not far from there that is useful if one does not mind swinging bridges over gorges with roaring water beneath.

"It is a very remote country, yet it seemed by far the best and far from troublesome officials. Who would expect to find anyone in such a place. Yet when we reached Chabrang—"

"Yes?"

"We went to a place where me might find food, and I heard a merchant, a Kirghiz, complaining in a loud voice against the government! He had been stopped, searched, questioned. It seemed there were soldiers there looking for someone with a great deal of money. As if any merchant dared carry any money at all in such a place!

"You can see my problem. But again I refused to be defeated! It is my decision that counts! I decided, and I acted! Promptly!

"I inquired, and in a voice just loud enough that all might hear, as to the ruins of Tsaparang and which road must I take?

"I knew the road, and I had seen the ruins. Who could forget them, high in that yellow cliff? Built into the very face of it like some of your cliff dwellings.

"Of course I knew where the ruins lay, and we went to them. The men I had hired to travel with me and who owned the horses were only too glad to lie in the shade and rest. I took a pack from a horse, some scientific instruments, and of course the money. Then I made my way up the steep slope. One too curious fellow chose to follow me, but I found heavy stones that must be moved from my path, so he soon lost interest.

"I hid the money, hid it securely, in a place only I shall find, and in its place I packed some broken bits of pottery, a few blue beads, bits of carnelian and such. I took measurements, and took pictures with an old camera I had wheedled from Milligan, and then returned to my horses.

"We were stopped, of course, and questioned. We were searched, and they found the shards of pottery, some butterflies collected long ago by that traveler, whoever he was, and some very smelly bottles.

"I had donned thick-lensed glasses with which I peered at them—I had to peer to see anything at all—and there, where they think much of the evil eye, they were pleased to be rid of me."

"And now you have been back? Did you pick up the money?"

He smiled. "One does what one must, lieutenant. Now I live here in Paris, and, I might say, I live well." He patted his stomach affectionately. "Even very well."

He sipped his wine. "Of course one must be careful when one has enemies. The old marshal—yes, he is alive and well—too well, altogether. He dislikes me for some reason. He would have me shot if he could. And regrettably there are others."

"What of the blonde? Milton's girl friend? Did you ever see her again?"

"See her?" He smiled complacently. "In fact, I shall see her tonight. I see her quite often, in fact."

"And the money? Milton's money?"

"She had taken it out of the black bag and hidden it.

But she was a fool! Did she spend it on beautiful clothes? Did she buy jewels and wine? She did not. She *invested* it, every centime! Invested it, can you imagine?"

He emptied his glass. "She invested in the black market. Somewhere she found truckloads of American cigarettes and tanks of petrol."

"So the quarter of a million is forever beyond your reach?"

"Did you say a quarter of a million? It is more than a million now, and only the good Lord knows where it will end! Given time, that stupid girl will own half of Paris."

I stood up. After all, I had things to do even if he did not, and as I turned to pick up my cap from an adjoining chair, there was a spiteful little snapping sound from beside me and a loud report from the door. Turning quickly, I saw the student, he who had been drinking coffee and working his sums at the outside table. The student had a Luger pistol that was slipping from his fingers, and as if by magic, the gendarmes were running into the court.

"Sit down, lieutenant." The general caught my arm, and holding it out from my body a little, guided me to a chair. "You cannot leave now. There will be questions."

Glancing out the door, I saw the student, or whatever he was, lying as he had fallen. Evidently he had spun when hit, for he lay face down almost in the doorway but headed the other way.

"Relax, lieutenant. It is nothing. The poor man! It is terrible, the kind of help one gets today! So inefficient!"

The police were there, questioning everybody, but of course nobody knew anything. We were the last.

The general spoke excellent French. "I am general—"

"We know, *mon général,* we know. Did you, by any chance, see what took place?"

"I did not, but you know how it is. The Free French are still finding pockets of resistance, and of course they are hunting collaborators. When they find them—" He held up his forefinger and thumb like a pistol. "When they find them—*ping!* And they deserve no better."

He stood up. "If you would like to search—?"

"Oh, no!" The gendarme was appalled. "Of course not, *mon général!* Of course not!"

When I reached my quarters that night, it was with some relief that I pulled off my tie and then started to shed my trench coat. Something bumped my side, and I slid my hand into the pocket—an automatic, small, neat, and very deadly.

It was not easy to be a friend of the general.

AUTHOR'S TEA

Each of us has a perception of the world and of man that is uniquely his own, yet some few have the gift of imparting that perception, of sharing with others their experience, their learning, and their understanding of the world in which we live. It is those few whom we read and read again, forever finding something new. None of us write as well as we should, and I the least of all.

Fiction enables a man to understand his world because it does not take a detached view. The author does not stand aloof and look upon people or conditions as does the philosopher, scientist, or historian. He gets inside the man, sees with his eyes, feels with his emotions.

Artists who work with the pen, brush, or chisel flatter themselves too much when they speak of creation, for his materials are here, all about him. What he does have is a gift of perception beyond the ordinary, for he must select from all this great mass that is life what is most useful for his purpose.

The rays of the world sun are diffused, the writer must bring all this into focus; he must see the whole, yet must recognize what is most useful for his purpose.

The art of creation is actually the art of skillful selection.

The process of creation is one that is little understood, although much studied. Even as the body's muscles can be trained to ultimate efficiency in the accomplishment of any athletic

feat, just so can the mind be conditioned for
creation. Each of us has stored within his sub-
conscious countless impressions, tastes, shad-
ings, experiences, and memories. It is probable
that nothing is ever completely lost, and the
writer can tap this inexhaustible storehouse of
recollection.

Yet to write well one must never cease from
learning, absorbing, observing, and sensing.
One can learn to organize the mind's filing sys-
tem for instant recall of whatever is essential
to the story.

As to writing, there are techniques to be learned,
skills to be acquired, as there is in any profession or trade. From the beginning of time, stories
have been told and over the millennia we have
learned how best to tell a story. Also, we have
found that stories fall into certain patterns of
behavior, which we call plots.

Many of those who comment on writing done
by others sometimes know surprisingly little
about writing itself and how it is done, and
often they speak of "plot" as something arti-
ficial. Nothing could be further from the truth.
Plots are nothing but constantly recurring human situations or patterns of behavior, and of
the twelve to eighteen plots on which 90 percent
of all fiction is based, they can be found in any
metropolitan newspaper in the course of any
given week.

The same plots that were used by the ancient
Greek dramatists were also used by Chaucer,
by Shakespeare, by Dickens, and by any con-
temporary writer of mysteries or of the West. It
is what is done with material in the develop-
ment of that plot that makes the difference. Nobody "invents" a plot. They are all here, hap-

pening every day, probably every hour. George
Polti, many years ago, listed thirty-six basic
plots, and nobody has ever improved on his list.
To offer an illustration of constantly recurring
plot patterns: at the moment of writing, the hos-
tage situation in Iran is much in the news. Here
we have a basic plot situation. A persecutor
(the so-called students), the suppliant (the hos-
tages), and the power in authority, Khomeini.
Another of these basic plots is the fugitive and
the pursuer, the theme of thousands of stories,
lately in the television serial "The Fugitive"
but also in Les Miserables. The most common
of all, perhaps, the wife or husband and two
adulterers.

As to my own writing, I cannot remember when
I was not trying to tell stories, certainly before I
ever went to school. Everybody thinks he can
tell a story well enough for publication, and I
certainly thought so. Most professional writers
have served an apprenticeship of about ten
years in learning their trade. Many people can
write one story, but to write many stories is
altogether a different thing. I often think that
the worst thing that can happen to a writer is to
have a big success with his first book. Unless he
or she has done much writing in other areas
before, the writer will never have learned his
trade.

The stories contained in this volume are largely
among the earliest stories I published, although
they were followed by many others. I had no
choice but to make a living as a writer, so I
wrote all kinds and types of stories; by far the
larger number were concerned with Asia, in one
aspect or another.

Many of my associates during the years when I

was working around over the West at whatever
job I could find were men and women who had
lived through the period of which I now write.
Gunfighters, gamblers, outlaws, and cowpunch-
ers did not live in some never-never land; they
were men who had to make a living, and they
worked, as I did, at whatever came to hand.
One whom I knew operated a small store, another a crossroads filling station.

My stories have come from incidents in my
own life, anecdotes I've hard, stories repeated
by miners, cowhands, Indians, and others whom
I've known.

"I'VE BEEN READING your work, Mr. Dugan, and like it tremendously! You have such *power*, such *feeling!*"

"Thank you," he heard himself saying. "I'm glad you liked it." He glanced toward the door where several women were arriving. They weren't young women. He sighed and glanced hopelessly toward the table where one of those faded dowagers who nibble at the crusts of culture was pouring tea. Now if they only had a steak—

"Mr. Dugan," his hostess was saying, "I want you to meet Mrs. Nowlin. She is also a writer."

She was so fat she had almost reached the parting of the stays, and she had one of those faces that always reminded him of buttermilk. "How do you do, Mrs. Nowlin?" He smiled in a way he hoped was gracious. "It is always a pleasure to meet someone in the same profession. What do you write?"

"Oh, I'm not a *regular* writer, Mr. Dugan, but I do so love to write! Don't you find it simply fascinating? But I just never have been able to get anything published. Sometimes I doubt the publishers even *read* my manuscripts! Why, I believe they just *couldn't!*"

"I imagine they are pretty busy, Mrs. Nowlin. They get so many stories, you know."

"Why, I sent one of my poems away not long ago. It was a poem about James, you know, and they wouldn't take it. They didn't even *say* anything! Just one of those rejection slips. Why, I read the poem at the club, and they all said it was simply *beautiful!*"

"Was—was James your husband?" he asked hopefully, glancing toward the tea table again. Still no steak.

"James! Oh, goodness no! James is my dog! My little Pom. Don't you just *adore* Poms, Mr. Dugan?"

Then she was gone, fluttering across the room like a blimp escaped from its moorings.

He sighed again. Every time chance caught him at one of these author's teas, he would think of Frisco Brady. He could imagine the profane disgust of the big Irish longshoreman if he knew the guy who flattened him in the Harbor Pool Room was guest of honor at a pink tea.

Dugan felt the red crawling around his ears at the thought, and his eyes sought the tea table again. Someday, he reflected, there is going to be a hostess who will serve real meals to authors and achieve immortality at a single stroke. Writers would burn candles to her memory, or better still, some of those shadowy wafers that were served with the tea and were scarcely more tangible than the tea itself.

He started out of his dream and tried to look remotely intelligent as he saw his hostess piloting another body through the crowd. He knew at a glance that she had written a book of poetry that wouldn't scan, privately published, of course. Even worse, it was obvious that in some dim, distant year she had seen some of Garbo's less worthy pictures and had never recovered. She carried her chin high, and her neck stretched endlessly toward affected shoulders.

"I have so *wanted* to meet you! There is something so deep, so spiritual about your work! And your last book! One feels you were on a great height when you wrote it! Ah! . . . ."

She was gone. But someone else was speaking to him, and he turned attentively.

"Why do so many of your writers write about such *hard* things? There is so much that is beautiful in the world! All people aren't like those people you write about, so why don't you write about *nice* people? And that boy you wrote about in the story about hunger, why, you know perfectly well, Mr. Dugan, that a boy like that couldn't go hungry in this country!"

His muscles ached with weariness, and he stood on the corner staring down the street, his thoughts blurred by hunger, his face white and strained. Somehow all form had become formless, and things about him took on new attitudes and appearances. He found his mind fastening upon little things with an abnormal concentration born of hunger and exhaustion. Walking a crack in the sidewalk became an obsession, and when he looked up from that, a fat man was crossing the street, and his arms and legs seemed to jerk grotesquely. Everything about him seemed to move in slow motion, and he stopped walking and tried to steady himself, conscious it was a delirium born of hunger.

He had been standing still for a moment trying to work his foot free from the sock where it was stuck with the dried blood from a broken blister, and when he moved forward suddenly, he almost fell. He pulled up sharply and turned his head to see if anyone noticed. He walked on then with careful attention.

He was hungry.

The words stood out in his consciousness, cold and clear, almost without thought or sensation. He looked at them as at a sign that had no meaning.

He passed a policeman and tried to adopt a careless, confident air but felt the man looking after him. Passing a bakery, the smell of fresh pastry went through him like a wave, leaving a sensation of emptiness and nausea.

"You've had such an *interesting* life, Mr. Dugan! There must have been so many adventures. If I had been a man, I would have lived just such a life as you have. It must have been so *thrilling* and romantic!"

"Why don't you tell us some of the *real* stories? Some of the things that actually happened? I'll bet there were a lot you haven't even written."

"I'm tellin' you, Dugan. Lay off that dame, see? If you don't, I'll cut your heart out."

The music moved through the room, and he felt the lithe, quick movements of the girl as she danced, and through the smoky pall he heard a chair crash, and he looked down and smiled at the girl, and then he spun her to arm's length and ducked to avoid the first punch. Then he struck with his left, short and hard. He felt his fist thud against a jaw and saw the man's face as he fell forward, eyes bulging, jaw slack. He brought up his right into the man's midsection as he fell toward him and then stepped away. Something struck him from behind, and it wasn't until he got up that the blood started running into his eyes. He knew he'd been hit hard, and he heard the music playing "In a little Spanish town 'twas on a night like this, stars were shining down . . ."

He was speaking then, and he heard himself saying, "There is only the personal continuity. The man we were yesterday may not be the man we are tomorrow. Names are only trademarks for the individual, and from day to day that individual changes, and his ways and thoughts change, although he is not always himself aware of the change. The man who was yesterday a soldier may be a seller of brushes tomorrow. He has the same name, but the man himself is not the same, although cicumstances may cause him to revert to his former personality and character. Even the body changes; the flesh and blood change with the food we eat and the water we drink.

"To him who drifts about, life consists of moving in and out of environments and changing conditions, and with each change of environment the wanderer changes, also. We move into lives that for the time are very near and dear to us, but suddenly all can be changed, and nothing remains but the memory.

"Only the innocent speak of adventure, for adventure is only a romantic name for trouble, and when one is having 'adventures' one wishes it were all over and he was elsewhere and safe. 'Adventure' is not nice. It is more often than not rough and dirty, cruel and harsh . . ."

Before they screwed on the copper helmet, Scotty stopped by, his features tight and hard. "Watch yourself, kid, this is bad water and too many sharks. Some say there are more octopi and squids here than anywhere else, but usually they're no trouble. We'll try to hold it down up here." He slapped his waistband as he spoke. Scotty moved, and Singapore Charlie lifted the helmet.

"Don't worry, skipper, I'll keep your lines clear, and I can handle any trouble." Then Dugan was sinking through the warm green water, feeling it clasp him close so that only the copper helmet protected him. Down, down, still farther down, and then he was standing on the sandy floor of the ocean, and around him moved the world of the undersea. There was silence, deep, unfathomable silence, except for the soft hiss of air. He moved forward, walking as though in a deep sleep, pushing himself against the water, turning himself from side to side like some unbelievable monster that haunted the lower depths.

Then he found the dark hull of the old ship and

moved along the ghostly deck, half shrouded in
the weed of a hundred years, moving toward the
companionway where feet no longer trod. He hesitated at the door, looking down into darkness,
and then he saw it moving toward him, huge,
ominous, frightening. He tucked his warm-
blooded hands into his armpits to leave only the
slippery surface of the canvas and rubber suit. It
came toward him, only vaguely curious, and in-
quiring tentacle slipped over and around him ...
feeling ... feeling ... feeling.

He sipped his tea and avoided the eyes of the
woman who had the manuscript she wanted him to
comment on, nibbled impotently at those infinitesimal
buttons of nourishment, and listened to the ebb and
flow of conversation about his ears. Here and there a
remark swirled about, attracting his momentary attention. He heard himself speaking, saying how pleasant
it had been, and then he was out on the street again,
turning up his collar against the first few drops of
spattering rain.

THE MOON OF THE TREES BROKEN BY SNOW:
A Christmas Story

"The Moon of the Trees Broken by Snow" (one translation of the Indian name for December) is a Christmas story about cliff dwellers who had never heard of Christmas and had never seen either a horse or a white man.

Sometime in the 1300s they vanished from their cliff dwellings, for which various reasons have been given. A few of them are in this story.

COLD BLEW THE WINDS along the canyon walls, moaning in the cedars, whining softly where the sage brush grew. Their fire was small, and they huddled close, the firelight playing shadow games on the walls, the walls their grandfather's father built when he moved from the pit house atop the mesa to the great arch of the shallow cave.

"We must go," the boy said, "for there is no more wood for burning, and the strength has gone from the earth. Our crops are thin, and when the snows have gone, the wild ones will come again, and they will kill us."

"It is so," his mother agreed. "One by one the others fled, and we are not enough to keep open the ditches that water our fields, nor to defend against the wild ones."

"Where will we go?" Small Sister asked.

They avoided looking at each other, their eyes hollow with fear, for they knew not where to go. Drought lay heavy upon the land, and from north, south, east, and west others had come seeking, no place seeming better than another. Was it not better to die here, where they had lived?

The boy was gaunt for each day he hunted farther afield and each day found less to hunt. Small Sister and his mother gathered brush or looted timbers from abandoned dwellings to keep their fires alight.

The Old One stirred and mumbled. "In my sleep I saw them," he muttered, "strange men sitting upon strange beasts."

"He is old," their mother said. "His thoughts wander."

How old he was they did not know. He had come out of the desert, and they cared for him. None knew what manner of man he was, but it was said he talked to gods, and they with him.

"Strange men," he said, "with robes that glisten."

"How many men?" The boy asked without curiosity but because he knew that to live, an old one must be listened to and questioned sometimes.

"Three," the Old One said, "no more."

Firelight flickered on the parchment of his ancient face. "Sitting upon beasts," he repeated.

Sitting upon? What manner of beast? And why sit upon them? The boy went to a corner for an old timber. A hundred years ago it had been a tree; now it was fuel.

They must leave or die, and it was better to die while doing than sitting. There was no corn left in the storage place. Even the rats were gone.

"When the light comes," the boy said, "we will go."

"What of the Old One? His limbs are weak."

"So are we all," the boy said. "Let him walk as far as he may."

"They followed a path," the Old One said, "a path where there was no path. They went where the light was."

On the third day their water was gone, but the boy knew of a seep. At the foot of the rocks he dug into the sand. When the sand grew damp, they held it against their brows, liking its coolness. Water seeped into the hollow, and one by one they drank.

They ate of the corn they carried, but some they must not eat. It would be seed for planting in the new place—if they found it.

During the night snow fell. They filled a water sack made of a skin and started on.

Within the morning the snow vanished. Here and there a few seeds still clung to the brush. Under an ironwood they rested, picking seeds from the ground. They could be parched and eaten or ground into pinole. As they walked they did not cease from looking, and the Old One found many seeds, although his eyes were bad.

"Where do we go?" Small Sister asked.

"We go," the boy replied, but inside he felt cold shivers as when one eats too much of the prickly-pear fruit. He did not know where they went, and he was much afraid.

On the ninth day they ate the last of their corn but for that which must be kept for seed. Twice the boy snarled ground squirrels, and three times he killed lizards. One day they stopped at a spring, gathering roots of a kind of wild potato the Pimas called *iikof*. His mother and the Old One dug them from the flat below the spring.

Day after day they plodded onward, and the cold grew. It snowed again, and this time it did not go away. The Old One lagged farther and farther behind, and each day it took him longer to reach the fire.

The boy did not meet their eyes now, for they looked to him, and he had nothing to promise.

"There was a path of light," the Old One muttered. "They followed the path."

He drew his worn blanket about his thin shoulders. "It is the Moon of the Limbs of Trees Broken by Snow," he whispered, "that was the time."

"What time, Old One?" The boy tried to be patient.

"The time of the path. They followed the path."

"We have seen no path, Old One."

"The path was light. No man had walked where the path lay."

"Why, then, did they follow? Were they fools?"

"They followed the path because they heard and they believed."

"Heard what? Believed in what?"

"I do not know. It came while I slept. I do not know what they believed, only that they believed."

"I believe we are lost," Small Sister said.

The mother looked to the boy. He was the man, although but a small man, and alone. "In the morning we will go on," he said.

The Old One arose. "Come," he said. Wondering, the boy followed.

Out in the night they went, stopping where no fire-light was. The Old One lifted his staff. "There!" he said. "There lies the path!"

"I see no path," the boy said, "only a star."

"The star is the path," the Old One said, "if you believe."

It was a bright star, hanging in the southern sky. The boy looked at it, and his lips trembled. He had but twelve summers. Yet he was the man, and he was afraid.

"The star is the path," the Old One said.

"There are many stars," the boy grumbled.

"The star was the path. They followed the star."

"How can one follow a star?" the boy protested.

The Old One went back to the fire and left the boy alone. They trusted him, and he did not trust himself. They had faith, and he had none. He led them into a wilderness—to what?

He had wandered, hoping. He had found nothing. He had longed, but the longing was empty. He found no place for planting, no food nor fuel.

He looked again. Was not that one star brighter than all the rest? Or did he only believe it so?

The Old One had said, "They followed a star."

He looked at the star. Then stepping back of a tall spear of yucca, he looked across it at the star. Then breaking off another spear, he set it in the sand and lined it up on the star so he would know the direction of the star when dawn came.

To lead them, he must believe. He would believe in the star.

When morning came, they took up their packs. Only the Old One sat withdrawn, unmoving. "It is enough," he said. "I can go no further."

"You will come. You taught me to have faith; you, too, must have it."

Day followed day, and night followed night. Each night the boy lined up his star with a peak, a tree, or a rock. On three of the days they had no food, and two days were without water. They broke the spines from cactus and sucked on the pulp from the thick leaves.

Small Sister's feet were swollen and the flesh broken. "It is enough," his mother said. "We can go no further."

They had come to a place where cottonwoods grew. He dug a hole in the stream bed and found a little water. They soaked cottonwood leaves and bound them to Small Sister's feet. "In the morning," he said, "we will go on."

"I cannot," Small Sister said.

With dead branches from the cottonwoods he built a fire. They broiled the flesh of a terrapin found on the desert. Little though there was, they shared it.

The boy walked out in the darkness alone. He looked up, and the star was there. "All right," he said.

When the light came, he shouldered his pack, and they looked at him. He turned to go, and one by one they followed. The Old One was the last to rise.

Now the land was broken by canyons. There was more cedar, occasionally a piñon. It snowed in the night, and the ground was covered, so they found only those seeds that still hung in their dry pods. They were very few.

Often they waited for the Old One. The walking was harder now, and the boy's heart grew small within him. At last they stopped to rest, and his mother looked at him: "It is no use. I cannot go on."

Small Sister said nothing and the Old One took a long time coming to where they waited.

"Do you stay, then?" the boy said. "I will go on."

"If you do not come back?"

"Then you are better without me," he said. "If I can, I will come."

Out of their sight he sat down and put his head in his hands. He had failed them. The Old One's medicine had failed. Yet he knew he must try. Small though he was, he was the man. He walked on, his thoughts no longer clear. Once he fell, and again he caught himself on a rock before falling. He straightened, blinking to clear his vision.

On the sand before him was a track, the track of a deer. He walked on and saw other tracks, those of a raccoon, and the raccoon liked water. Not in two months had he seen the track of an animal. They led away down the canyon.

He went out on the rocks and caught himself abruptly, almost falling over the rim. It was a limestone sink, and it was filled with water. He took up a stone and dropped it, and it hit the pool and sank with a deep, rich, satisfying sound. The well was deep and wide, with a stream running from one side.

He went around the rim and lay down flat to drink of the stream. Something stirred near him, and he looked up quickly.

They were there: his mother, Small Sister, and the Old One. He stood up, very straight, and he said, "This is our place; we will stop here."

The boy killed a deer, and they ate of it. He wiped his fingers on his buckskin leggings and said, "Those who sat upon the beasts? What did they find, following their star?"

"A cave that smelled of animals where a baby lay on dry grass. The baby's father and mother were there, and some other men wearing skins, who stood by with bowed heads."

"And the shining ones who sat upon beasts?"

"They knelt before the baby and offered it gifts."

"It is a strange story," the boy said, "and at another time I will listen to it again. Now we must think of planting."

LET ME FORGET ...

Let me forget the dark seas rolling.
The taste of wind, the lure and lift
Of far, blue shrouded shores;
No longer let the wild wind's singing
Build high the waves in this
My heart's own storm;
Now let me quietly work, for I have songs.
Let not my blood beat answer to the sea ...
The beaches lie alone, so let them lie.
Let me forget the gray-banked distant hills,
The echoing emptiness of ancient towns;
No longer let the brown leaves falling
Move me to wander ... I have songs to sing.

ABOUT LOUIS L'AMOUR

"I think of myself in the oral tradition—as a troubadour, a village taleteller, the man in the shadows of the campfire. That's the way I'd like to be remembered—as a storyteller. A good storyteller."

It is doubtful that any author could be as at home in the world re-created in his novels as Louis Dearborn L'Amour. Not only could he physically fill the boots of the rugged characters he wrote about, but he literally "walked the land my characters walk." His personal experiences as well as his lifelong devotion to historical research combined to give Mr. L'Amour the unique knowledge and understanding of people, events, and the challenge of the American frontier that became the hallmarks of his popularity.

Of French-Irish descent, Mr. L'Amour could trace his own family in North America back to the early 1600s and follow their steady progression westward, "always on the frontier." As a boy growing up in Jamestown, North Dakota, he absorbed all he could about his family's frontier heritage, including the story of his great-grandfather who was scalped by Sioux warriors.

Spurred by an eager curiosity and desire to broaden his horizons, Mr. L'Amour left home at the age of fifteen and enjoyed a wide variety of jobs including seaman, lumberjack, elephant handler, skinner of dead cattle, assessment miner, and officer on tank destroyers during World War II. During his "yondering" days he also circled the world on a freighter, sailed a dhow on the Red Sea, was shipwrecked in the West Indies and stranded in the Mojave Desert. He won fifty-one of fifty-nine fights as a professional boxer and worked as a journalist and lecturer. He was a voracious reader and collector of rare books. Mr. L'Amour's personal library of some 10,000 volumes covers a broad range of scholarly disciplines including many personal papers, maps, and diaries of the pioneers.

Mr. L'Amour "wanted to write almost from the time I could talk." After developing a widespread following for his many adventure stories written for fiction magazines, Mr. L'Amour published his first full-length novel, *Hondo*, in the United States in 1953. Every one of his more than 100 books is in print; there are nearly 200 million copies of his books in print worldwide, making him one of the bestselling authors in modern literary history. His books have been translated into twenty languages, and more than forty-five of his novels and stories have been made into feature films and television movies.

His hardcover bestsellers include *The Lonesome Gods*, *The Walking Drum* (his twelfth-century historical novel), *Jubal Sackett*, *Last of the Breed*, and *The Haunted Mesa*.

The recipient of many great honors and awards, in 1983 Mr. L'Amour became the first novelist ever to be awarded the National Gold Medal by the United States Congress in honor of his life's work. In 1984 he was also awarded the Medal of Freedom by President Reagan.

Louis L'Amour died on June 10, 1988. His wife, Kathy, and their two children, Beau and Angelique, carry the L'Amour tradition forward.

1. ☐ WAR PARTY   25393 $2.95
☐ Trap of Gold ☐ One for the Pot ☐ War Party ☐ Get Out of Town ☐ Booty for a Badman ☐ The Gift of Cochise ☐ A Mule for Santa Fe ☐ Alkali Basin ☐ Men to Match the Hills ☐ The Defense of Sentinel

2. ☐ THE STRONG SHALL LIVE   25200 $2.95
☐ The Strong Shall Live ☐ One-Night Stand ☐ Trail to Squaw Springs ☐ Merrano of the Dry Country ☐ The Romance of Piute Bill ☐ Hattan's Castle ☐ Duffy's Man ☐ Big Man ☐ The Marshal of Sentinel ☐ Bluff Creek Station

3. ☐ YONDERING   26039 $2.95
☐ Where There's Fighting ☐ The Dancing Kate ☐ Glorious! ☐ Dead-End Drift ☐ Old Doc Yak ☐ Survival ☐ Thicker Than Blood ☐ The Admiral ☐ Shanghai Not Without Gestures ☐ The Man Who Stole Shakespeare ☐ A Friend of the General ☐ Author's Tea ☐ A Man of the Trees Broken by Snow

4. ☐ BUCKSKIN RUN   24764 $2.95
☐ The Ghosts of Buckskin Run ☐ No Trouble for the Cactus Kid ☐ Horse Heaven ☐ Squatters on the Lonetree ☐ Jackson of Horntown ☐ There's Always a Trail ☐ Down the Pogonip Trail ☐ What Gold Does to a Man

5. ☐ BOWDRIE   23368 $2.95
☐ Bowdrie Rides a Coyote Trail ☐ A Job for a Ranger ☐ Bowdrie Passes Through ☐ A Trail to the West ☐ More Brains Than Bullets ☐ Too Tough to Brand ☐ The Thriller From the Pecos

6. ☐ THE HILLS OF HOMICIDE   24134 $2.95
☐ The Hills of Homicide ☐ Unguarded Moment ☐ Dead Man's Trail ☐ With Death in His Corner ☐ The Street of Lost Corpses ☐ Stay Out of My Nightmare ☐ Collect From a Corpse ☐ I Hate to Tell His Widow

7. ☐ BOWDRIE'S LAW   24550 $2.95
☐ McNelly Knows a Ranger ☐ Where Buzzards Fly ☐ Case Closed—No Prisoners ☐ Down Sonora Way ☐ The Road to Casa Piedras ☐ A Ranger Rides to Town ☐ South of Deadwood ☐ The Outlaws of Poplar Creek ☐ Rain on the Mountain Fork ☐ Strange Pursuit

8. ☐ LAW OF THE DESERT BORN 24133 $2.95
☐ Law of the Desert Born ☐ Riding On ☐ The Black Rock Coffin Makers ☐ Desert Death Songs ☐ Ride, You Tonto Raiders! ☐ One Last Gun Notch ☐ Death Song of the Sombrero ☐ The Guns Talk Loud ☐ Grub Line Rider ☐ The Marshal of Painted Rock ☐ Trap of Gold

9. ☐ RIDING FOR THE BRAND 26189 $2.95
☐ Riding for the Brand ☐ Four-Card Draw ☐ His Brother's Debt ☐ A Strong Land Growing ☐ The Turkeyfeather Riders ☐ Lit a Shuck for Texas ☐ The Nester and the Piute ☐ Barney Takes a Hand ☐ Man Riding West ☐ Fork Your Own Broncs ☐ Home in the Valley ☐ West Is Where the Heart Is

10. ☐ DUTCHMAN'S FLAT 26189 $2.95
☐ Dutchman's Flat ☐ Keep Travelin' Rider ☐ Trail to Pie Town ☐ Mistakes Can Kill You ☐ Big Medicine ☐ Man From Battle Flat ☐ West of the Tularosas ☐ McQueen of the Tumbling K ☐ The One for the Mohave Kid ☐ The Lion Hunter and the Lady ☐ A Gun for Kilkenny

11. ☐ THE RIDER OF THE RUBY HILLS 26393 $2.95
☐ The Rider of the Ruby Hills ☐ Showdown Trail ☐ A Man Called Trent ☐ The Trail to Peach Meadow Canyon

12. ☐ THE TRAIL TO CRAZY MAN 26392 $2.95
☐ The Trail to Crazy Man ☐ Riders of the Dawn ☐ Showdown on the Hogback

13. ☐ NIGHT OVER THE SOLOMONS 26602 $2.95
☐ Night Over the Solomons ☐ Mission to Siberut ☐ Pirates With Wings ☐ Tailwind to Tibet ☐ The Goose Flies South ☐ Wings Over Khabarovsk

14. ☐ WEST FROM SINGAPORE 26353 $2.95
☐ East of Gorontalo ☐ On the Road to Amurang ☐ From Here to Banggai ☐ The House of Qasavara ☐ Well of the Unholy Light ☐ West From Singapore ☐ South of Suez

15. ☐ LONIGAN 27536 $3.50
☐ Lonigan ☐ Regan of the Slash B ☐ Heritage of Hate ☐ Rowdy Rides to Glory ☐ Pardner from Rio ☐ Bill Carey Rides West

---

Bantam Books, Dept. LL23, 414 East Golf Road, Des Plaines, IL 60016

Please send me the books I have checked above. I am enclosing $_____ (please add $2.00 to cover postage and handling). Send check or money order—no cash or C.O.D.s please.

Mr/Ms _____

Address _____

City/State _____ Zip _____

LL23—10/88

Please allow four to six weeks for delivery. This offer expires 4/89. Prices and availability subject to change without notice.